Dear Reader,

Here we are, back in Good Riddance, Alaska, where folks get to leave behind what ails them.

And former marine sniper Liam Reinhardt really needs to move on. Behind him, he's left a career, a wife and a sense of purpose. And he's mad as hell.

Tansy Wellington needs a new start too. She's leaving behind a cheating fiancé and a job she's not sure she can do anymore. Needless to say, she's none too happy either.

For both Liam and Tansy, Good Riddance starts off as a sanctuary…and then turns into much, much more.

What they both quickly learn is that sometimes people have to discover their own path in life before thinking about moving forward with a partner. Sometimes even the best-laid plans get derailed. When one door closes, another one opens—all we have to do is notice it. Lucky for us, Tansy and Liam soon notice that other door…and delight in the fact that it leads to the bedroom!

I hope you enjoy the sparks that fly between this hotheaded (and hot-blooded) couple. And remember, always keep an eye out for that open door. You never know what you might find…

I'd love to hear from you. Please drop me a note at Jennifer@jenniferlabrecque.com. And, as always, happy reading!

Jennifer LaBrecque

NORTHERN
RENEGADE

BY
JENNIFER LABRECQUE

Harlequin (UK) policy is to use papers that are natural, renewable and recyclable products and made from wood grown in sustainable forests. The logging and manufacturing processes conform to the legal environmental regulations of the country of origin.

Printed and bound in Spain
by Blackprint CPI, Barcelona

MILLS
BOON

First published in Great Britain 2012
by Mills & Boon, an imprint of Harlequin (UK) Limited,
Eton House, 18-24 Paradise Road, Richmond, Surrey TW9 1SR

© Jennifer LaBrecque 2012

ISBN: 978 0 263 89745 6

30-1112

After a varied career path that included barbecue-joint waitress, corporate number-cruncher and bug-business maven, **Jennifer LaBrecque** has found her true calling writing contemporary romance. Named 2001 Notable New Author of the Year and 2002 winner of a prestigious Maggie Award for Excellence, she is also a two-time RITA® Award finalist. Jennifer lives in suburban Atlanta with a Chihuahua who runs the whole show.

ACKNOWLEDGEMENT

Many thanks to Gervais Cranston for sharing his
expertise, passion and respect for weapons…
and the time and instruction at the firing range.

1

GUNNERY SERGEANT LIAM Reinhardt, former United States Marines sharpshooter, veered his motorcycle to the left, avoiding another pothole in the pockmarked gravel road. It wasn't much better than the goat trails leading from one remote Afghani village to the next. Except, this wasn't Afghanistan and he wasn't tracking some insurgent leader through dusty mountains.

Nope, he was back in the U.S. of A. Afghanistan, Iraq and some places he couldn't divulge were his past. As was his ex-wife and an honorable discharge based on some faulty heart valve that had shown up when he was being patched up from that last mission. That assignment had been the pinnacle of his career. It was right up there with the SEALs taking out bin Laden back in 2011, only Liam's mission had had a lower profile.

Growing up, hunting in the woods of Minnesota and Wisconsin, he'd known early on he wanted to be a sharpshooter. The irony wasn't lost on him that while he'd been fully prepared that enemy fire might take him out at any time, he'd never expected to lose his life, as he knew it, due to a personal plumbing defect.

Neither had he planned on Natalie bailing on their marriage two years ago because she couldn't handle his deployments. What the hell? She'd known his career path when she married him. Now it was time to regroup because all of that was history. At thirty-one, he was starting all over. Starting what? Doing what? He'd be damned if he knew.

Rolling to a stop, he pushed up his helmet's bug-spattered visor and surveyed his immediate future. Good Riddance, Alaska, spread before him. A single road cut through the collection of buildings flanked at the rear by evergreens.

Over the throb of his bike, he heard the drone of a plane. Bush plane. It was a far cry from the sound of F-15s and recon drones or the fractured *chop-chop-chop* of a Chinook. Sure enough, a bush plane, coming in low, touched down on the landing strip to the right of the town.

A breeze carried the scent of spruce and the odor of bear. While the trees were everywhere, bears would remain scarce. For the most part, they avoided people. He knew the feeling. He wanted to be left the hell alone.

Back home in Minnesota, that had been damn near impossible with his mom hovering over him. He and she operated on different planes, and after his dad died, their differences had seemed more marked than ever.

Liam craved the solitude he remembered from when he'd visited Good Riddance as a teenager. And his uncle, Bull Swenson, a tough-as-nails vet who'd spent some time in a Vietcong hellhole back in 'Nam, had found a new start and a new life here. Liam had followed in Bull's footsteps joining the military. He figured he might as well follow Bull's lead afterward, as well. Good Riddance seemed like an all-around good decision—or at least a decent enough option to make it worth checking out.

Flipping his visor back into place, Liam rolled out once again. Within minutes and a mile or so, the piece of crap road had widened. It was certainly no mystery as to why the bush pilots had plenty of business.

On the outskirts of town, a group of kids played baseball in a clearing. Not the Little League stuff his ex-wife's nephews had played with tricked-out uniforms, brow-knitted coaches and overbearing, yelling parents. There hadn't been a thing fun about it for the kids as far as he could tell the couple of times Natalie had dragged him along to watch. Nah. He grinned. This was good old "sandlot" ball.

He caught a couple of curious glances as he parked his bike in front of the long log building on the edge of town that was both the air center, bed-and-breakfast and the only joint that sold a hot meal and a cold drink. Chances were Bull was in either the restaurant or the airstrip office instead of his hardware company.

Liam stood, feeling the stretch in his legs and back, although maintaining one position for hours was old hat to him. It was what he'd trained for and had done for a long time.

He pulled off his helmet and hung it on the handlebars, the breeze feeling good against his head. Two kids, a boy and a girl, both blond and freckled, with a sled dog at their side, sans sled, stopped on the sidewalk and eyed Liam's motorcycle with a mix of admiration and envy.

"That's a sweet ride," the boy said. Liam figured they were about seven or eight.

Liam smiled at the kid's terminology. That was one thing he'd learned—boys were boys and they liked boy toys whether it was the Middle East or suburban Minnesota or the Alaskan bush. Boss Black, as he called his Benelli, *was* damn sweet with an 1131 cc engine, matte black paint and plenty of chrome. "Thanks. I like it."

The girl piped up. "I like your helmet."

The boy rolled his eyes. "Girls."

"Shut up." She landed an elbow to his side.

Liam smiled. "Let me guess—brother and sister?"

The girl spoke up. "Twins." She shot her brother a triumphant smirk. "I'm the oldest."

That pulled a laugh out of Liam. "Me, too. I beat my brother out by five minutes." And much like this kid, he never let Lars forget it.

She looked slightly crestfallen. "Oh, I was only four minutes," she perked up, "but I was still first."

"That's because they were saving the best for last," the boy said. Obviously they'd run through this spiel a number of times before.

"Humph."

"Our grandparents run the dry goods store," the boy said, ignoring his sister's disdainful snort. "We're spending the summer with them. They can hook you up if you need stuff. The beef jerky's really good. Mr. Curl makes it himself."

"Thanks, I'll keep that in mind."

A whoop came from the baseball game down the way. "I'm playing first base."

"Uh-uh. Me."

They exchanged a look Liam recognized from swapping the same look with his twin brother, Lars, innumerable times—*not if I get there first.*

"See ya," they yelled in unison as they took off running, the dog loping down the sidewalk behind them.

The town had definitely grown since the last time he was here, which would've been sixteen or so years ago when he was sixteen and still wet behind the ears. But it still had a good feel to it. He opened the door and walked into the bed-and-breakfast/airfield office.

It was pretty much the way he remembered it. Lace-trimmed flannel curtains still hung at the windows. A couple of tables were in "the front room." The far side wall definitely held more framed photographs but the potbellied stove was still flanked by a couple of rocking chairs with a chess and checkers table between two of them.

In the far corner, a flat-screened television had replaced the older boxy model that had been there. The armchair and love seat also had a newer look than he remembered. But it still felt and smelled the same—welcoming.

Merilee Danville Weatherspoon turned from her desk to the right of the back door leading to the airstrip.

"Hi there, Merilee."

Within seconds recognition dawned in her blue eyes and a broad welcoming smile lit her face. "Liam!"

She pushed up from her desk and crossed the room, her arms already extended to embrace him. She enfolded him in a welcoming hug, giving him a squeeze. "It's so good to see you! We knew you were coming, but we didn't know when."

"That makes two of us. I took my time getting here."

"Does Bull know you're here?"

He shook his head. "I figured he was either here or next door and I knew for sure coffee was here so…"

Merilee smiled as she turned and headed for the coffee stand. Within seconds she'd poured him a cup. She was damn near as fast with that coffeepot as he was with his Glock. "Straight up?"

"Always." He grinned as he took the cup from her. That's how he preferred any situation—straight up.

"Muffin?"

"No, thanks."

"That's right. I remember you don't have a sweet tooth at all. You're looking good."

He laughed. "I need a shave and a haircut, but thanks." She was a classy lady and it was a nice thing to say. "You're looking good yourself."

"Well, thank you. That's because I'm happy. Bull and I got married."

"Congratulations! That's cool."

"It has been very cool," she said. She practically glowed.

The cynical side of him was impressed. Merilee and Bull had been an item for a damn long time. It was pretty mind-blowing she could still look like that, all soft and sweet, when she talked about his uncle. He wouldn't rain on her happy parade but her talk of marriage inevitably led him to think of his own marriage... and subsequent divorce.

Liam supposed, in retrospect, he'd never felt that way about Natalie and obviously she sure as hell hadn't felt that way about him. He'd liked being married but the truth was he hadn't missed Natalie as much per se as he'd missed having someone to come home to. And it had been a long time since he'd had a woman. Since his divorce, a few had come on to him and he'd even briefly considered an uncomplicated exchange of sex for money when a hooker had propositioned him, but he'd passed on all of it. He'd been beyond that mindless physical engagement back in his early twenties.

"How long have you guys been married?" he said.

"It'll be two years in December. We tied the knot on Christmas Day. I'll let Bull tell you the story." She grinned. "I just wanted to tell you the news."

He liked Merilee even more now than he had when he was a teenager. Although, he'd thought she was pretty damn cool then, too. She'd left her old man, driven an RV out to nowhere and founded a damn town. Now that was a woman with a pioneer spirit. Back in the day, she'd been the town mayor. He'd bet a buck she still was.

"You still the mayor?"

She nodded. "I can't find anyone to run against me. At this point it feels more like dictator-for-life." She rolled her eyes. "I've thought about stepping down so I could just relax and Bull and I could travel, but it hasn't worked out that way."

"Not your style. You're a born leader."

She grinned. "Bull says I like to have my own way. He just stepped next door to Gus's if you want to drop in over there. I imagine you're ready for a hot meal."

"I could eat a bite or two." He could get by on field rations but he enjoyed a home-cooked meal as much as the next man. Well, maybe a little more. His last real meal had been when he pulled out of Anchorage a couple of days ago. "Whatever's cooking next door smells good."

"Caribou potpie. Lucky, the guy who owns it now, does a good job."

It smelled damn good, that was for sure. "I'll go check it out and catch up with Bull." He smiled and turned to head for the restaurant that adjoined the airstrip center.

Merilee spoke, halting him. "Liam…" He turned. Smiling, she said, "Welcome to Good Riddance, where you get to leave behind what ails you."

"Thanks." Unfortunately, it wasn't that simple and he wasn't sure that was why he was here.

BASTARD. BASTARD. BASTARD.

The words had danced around in her brain all morning like some liturgical chant…which made it altogether fairly difficult to make progress on her book, which was due at the publisher's at the end of the month. And actually fairly difficult to concentrate on what her stepsister, Jenna, was saying now.

Jenna waved a hand in front of Tansy's face. "Woohoo! Hello there. Anyone home? Earth to Tansy."

Tansy shook her head to clear it and laughed, focusing on Jenna's teasing countenance across the booth of Gus's, the only restaurant in Good Riddance. It was a fun mix of a saloon from an old Western and a downhome diner. She and Jenna were sitting in a booth near the bar and front door. A mounted moose head overlooked the bar, which boasted a brass foot rail. The other side of the room held more booths and tables, a jukebox, a dartboard and a couple of pool tables. Regardless of the time of day, in the week that Tansy had been here, the local gathering spot was never without customers. "Sorry. I was wool-gathering."

"BB?"

It was simply embarrassing to admit she was allowing him to eat up her brain space. Nonetheless, Tansy nodded her head. They had dubbed Bradley, Tansy's former fiancé, Bradley the Butthead or Bradley the Bastard, which she had subsequently shortened to BB.

"Yes. Stupid, huh? He's just been on my brain this morning."

Jenna's blue eyes reflected sympathetic understanding. "I wouldn't call it stupid. I'd call it human. You guys have been an item since junior high school. He's the only guy you ever dated, the only guy you ever… well, you know. He inspired your column, your book. He's been your past, your present and, you thought, your future. I think I'd be more worried about you if he wasn't invading your thoughts."

As usual, Jenna made her own kind of sense.

"Well, technically, you know he's not the only guy I ever dated. Remember? We broke up for a while our freshman year in college?"

"You went out for pizza with one guy and the movies with another one. Once. That really doesn't count as dating."

Tansy stirred her spoon in her coffee cup idly.

"I guess."

Tansy had met Bradley in seventh grade. He had been her one and only. Those couple of dates with other guys had been enough for Tansy. She and Bradley had gotten back together from then on. Last Christmas he'd asked her to marry him. They'd done everything right. They'd moved forward cautiously, taken their time, made plans…and look where they'd wound up— Splitsville.

Heck, their history had sort of spawned her career as a love advice blogger and columnist. And then she'd started a book, *Finding Your Own Fairy-tale Ending,* that had been bought by a publisher. The book was slated for a February release, just in time for Valentine's Day, and now she was floundering because everything she'd thought she'd known about love and relationships had been turned on its ear with Bradley's infidelity. Coming to Good Riddance had been a good move on her part as she tried to find her footing with both the book and her life.

"Coming here has helped," she said.

Jenna had been totally enthusiastic when Tansy had proposed coming to Alaska for a change of venue. Plus, she'd been dying to meet her new niece, Emma. And there was the little matter of having to get this book finished.

Jenna offered a sage nod. "Yep. Good Riddance… where you get to leave behind what ails you. It's all going to be okay, Tansy."

Tansy and Jenna had been thirteen when their parents had married. The girls had formed a quick bond. Not only were they the same age but they both had parents who were addicts. However, rather than drugs or alcohol, their parents had been marriage addicts. Divorce always seemed to lead to finding the next "fix." If there was such a thing as serial spouses, Jenna's mom and Tansy's dad, to a much lesser extent, were case-book studies.

Tansy and Jenna had shared a bedroom when Tansy spent time at her dad's. Tansy had long ago come to regard Jenna as her true sister and her friend. Most of the time she didn't bother with the "step" designation and simply referred to Jenna as her sister. Not surprisingly, their parents' marriage hadn't lasted more than two years—just long enough for the new to wear off—and then Jenna's mom and Tansy's dad were off to greener grasses. Jenna and Tansy had stayed in touch, and although there were inevitable ebbs and flows in their relationship, they remained close.

"I feel like an idiot," Tansy said, impatient with herself, "wallowing in man-woes." She had never been one to wallow.

"You're not an idiot and you're not wallowing." Jenna's eyes flashed. "You found a pair of panties—not yours—in your fiancé's jacket pocket. And then there were the emails and the hotel receipt." God, she'd been painfully stupid and trusting. "There'd be something wrong with you if you weren't having days like this."

Tansy supposed. Sometimes she did okay and then sometimes it was like this. It wasn't even as if she was totally brokenhearted. She was just…pissed. Why tell her he loved her? Why ask her to marry him if he was going to be fooling around with someone else? Not only was the bastard wrecking her concentration, worse, he'd made her feel like a fraud. How could she offer up advice on love and relationships when hers had hit the skids and she was still a mess? She wrote a syndicated column, had a wildly successful webpage and her own love life was in the toilet? Small wonder she'd stalled on the book she'd been working on. She hadn't lost just her fiancé, it had been a whole damn belief in something bigger.

Admittedly, she liked it here—actually she loved it here—and it was wonderful to be with Jenna and Emma, who was cute as a bug. But Tansy had made precious little progress on her book and felt bogus every time she wrote her column. "I'll figure it out."

"You will." Jenna shook her blond head while she waved at someone across the room. "Coming here was a good thing. It would've been a million times worse if you were still in Chattanooga. We're glad you're here, even if you are in solitary confinement most of the time."

Jenna's husband, Logan, had offered Tansy the use of his new FJ Cruiser. Jenna had reassured her that Logan would never have offered it if he didn't want Tansy to drive it. So, she was staying out at a little recently renovated cabin at a place called Shadow Lake. Outside of visits to her grandfather's farm halfway between Chattanooga and Marietta, Tansy had never done remote. She'd always lived in the city. She found she rather liked it, especially as she drove in at least once a day for a meal at Gus's or Jenna's.

And while it was nice and tranquil, Bradley remained a thorn in her side…or brain, rather. And the clock kept ticking. She had two weeks to push through to the end and then it was time to head back home and deliver her book to her publisher. She was nearing meltdown mode. She put down her fork. The food was delicious but she'd lost her appetite. Tansy wasn't one to stay down for long, which made this all so confounding and annoying. "The book has to be written."

"I know. And it's pretty hard to write relationship advice when your heart is breaking…or you're still going through whatever." Jenna patted her hand across the table. "It'll all work out. Really it will. And I hate to run but I've got to get back. Nancy's got an appointment and she only wants me, plus I need to check on Emma and her daddy."

Jenna was one of those people who had been consistently underestimated. Even though she came across as slightly spacey—Tansy had even heard her referred to as a dumb blonde when they were in high school, which she had always quickly corrected—Jenna had a terrific head for business. In the year and a half she'd been in Good Riddance she'd started a small nail business, which had grown into a day spa, with her living quarters above it. Jenna was very much a hands-on owner and a seize-the-moment personality whereas Tansy was a planner and strategizer. Consequently, having things fall through with Bradley had totally thrown her for a loop. Maybe she should borrow a page from Jenna and be a little more open to spontaneity. Hey, she was here, wasn't she and that had been a fairly spontaneous decision.

"I'm glad I'm here," Tansy said. "It's wonderful to meet you for lunch and be a part of your life…and spoil my niece."

Although, three-month-old Emma Evangeline Jeffries rather scared Tansy. Emma was so little and perfect, it was almost frightening. And Tansy thought it was charming that Jenna's husband, Logan, wasn't just besotted with both his wife and daughter, but actively participated in Emma's care. The CFO of his family's mining firm, he made time to watch Emma while Jenna ran the day spa.

Sometimes seeing Jenna and Logan and their little family together made Tansy realize just how off the mark her and Bradley's relationship had been, even without the panties in his pocket and the incriminating emails.

"Come over for dinner and a movie tonight. I'm not cooking." Jenna laughed reassuringly. "Logan's got the Crock-Pot fired up." Jenna's lack of cooking skills were legendary, both back in Georgia and now throughout

Alaska. While Tansy simply didn't like to cook, Jenna couldn't seem to master it. Tansy smiled. "And we're watching *Tangled* on DVD. You know you like that movie." Tansy was a sucker for romantic fairy tales, as was evidenced by the title of her book. Now she didn't know what fairy tale, if any, was in her future. "Maybe that's what you need to lift you out of your writer's-block funk. It's a cute romance."

It was sweet of Jenna to include Tansy but sometimes seeing Jenna's little family just made the whole thing with Bradley that much more painful. That's what she had wanted. That's what she had thought she was getting. "Let me see where I am."

"What you need is a good healthy dose of a real man."

In a moment of spectacular timing, Rooster McFie practically crowed from his spot across the restaurant/bar/pool hall. The shock of red hair and beard weren't the only aspects that had earned him the Rooster moniker. He had the most disconcerting habit of almost crowing when he was excited. Dear God, she couldn't imagine what he must be like when he was in the throes of sexual fulfillment. Ugh. It was one of those things she really didn't want to imagine but crowded into her brain regardless.

Truthfully, she was all kinds of open to a sweet, gentle knight showing up on a figurative white steed—yes, she was a hopeless romantic—but she simply wasn't seeing that happening in a small town in the middle of Alaska.

"I'm not holding my breath."

Jenna looked past Tansy, and a slow smile bloomed

on her face. "Don't look now, but I believe that man is just what the doctor ordered."

Don't look now had to be one of the worst phrases because it fairly begged you to do just that.

She looked…and couldn't seem to look away as something hot and real and slightly dangerous seemed to slam into her and through her, leaving her breathless and shaken.

Tansy didn't know *who* he was, but she definitely knew, at first glance, precisely *what* he was—tall, lean, dark, wounded, inaccessible and somewhere the other side of sexy.

She finally looked away, feeling flushed and disheveled, as if he'd touched her, run his fingers through her hair, brushed against her skin, marked her in some way.

She also knew exactly what he wasn't. This stranger was definitely no gentle knight on a white steed.

2

LIAM SCANNED THE ROOM for Bull. Sixteen years wouldn't render his uncle unrecognizable. Even though he wasn't a tall or loud man, Bull Swenson was a man of presence. Gus's was nearly full, though, so Liam continued to search the crowded room.

And then, suddenly he saw her midscan, across the room. The hair on the back of his neck stood at attention. Short dark hair. Glasses. Slightly round face. Average height. Lavender T-shirt. Her eyes locked with his.

It was as if everything slowed down inside him, the same way it did when he was about to take a shot. His heart rate slowed. His breath stilled for several counts.

And then she turned around and the rest of the room came back into focus. He wasn't sure what the hell had just happened, but something had. He felt shaken and there was very little that shook his composure. It was as if she'd sighted him in her crosshairs.

He mentally shook his head, dismissing the feeling, and continued his scan. Bull. Four o'clock. At the bar.

Bull looked Liam's way and without a word to the guy sitting next to him, stood. Liam met his uncle halfway. Bull's handshake turned into a one-armed hug. "You made it."

There was a whole hell of a lot that went unsaid in those three words. Bull wasn't just talking about Liam arriving in Good Riddance. It was an acknowledgment from one soldier who'd survived combat to another.

"I did."

"I'm glad you're here. It's a good place to be."

For the first time in a long time Liam felt as if he could exhale, at least a little. He still didn't know what the hell he was going to do with his life but for now, being here felt right.

"Yeah, it seems to have treated you well."

Liam had seen some things—terrible things, but it was nothing compared to Bull's experience. As a POW in Vietnam, Bull had been to hell and back.

Bull grinned. "Can't complain, can't complain. Nice job on that mission. How's the leg?"

Liam shrugged it off. "Not a problem." The only problem had been when they'd been patching up what was little more than a flesh wound they'd found his faulty heart valve. That was the damned problem, not his leg.

Bull simply nodded and moved on to ask, "You hungry?"

Liam grinned. "Damn near starving."

"Then belly up to the bar and we'll feed you while you meet everyone."

Throughout the entire exchange with Bull, Liam had had an undercurrent of awareness, always sensing the presence of the woman sitting in the booth to his left. He would find out who she was, but he'd wait until Bull had made introductions and see if one was forthcom-

ing. Two characteristics had been honed by his training, his instinct and patience. He could wait, but in the
meantime he was cognizant of her.

Several minutes later he felt as if he'd met damn
near everyone in the joint…except *her*. However, the
blonde at the booth with her, a woman named Jenna,
had stopped by on her way out. Liam now knew the
other woman's name. Tansy. Tansy Wellington. She was
Jenna's sister and was here visiting from Chattanooga.

He'd never met anyone named Tansy. But he'd also
never reacted that way to a woman, either. In an instant
she'd slid beneath his skin. It wasn't as if his guard was
down because his guard was a permanent fixture. Nope,
she'd just slipped in, marched straight through and set
up camp. He didn't like it a damn bit.

A tall, raw-boned woman plunked a plate heaped
with a healthy portion of potpie on the counter before him. "Thanks," he said with a nod, picking up his
spoon. He turned to Bull. "So, congratulations. Merilee
says the two of you tied the knot."

He took a bite. The potpie was damn good.

"Yep. When you find a good woman you've got
to hold on to her, even if you have to spend twenty-
something years to pin her down."

Liam spoke frankly to Bull. They'd always had that
kind of relationship, even though they didn't see each
other often. Both of them were straight shooters. "I'm
surprised you and Merilee married after all this time."

"Yeah? Well, that's because the crazy woman was
still married, but just hadn't mentioned that minor de-
tail. Hell, I've been trying to marry her since I met her.
When you find a good one you have to keep her."

"No kidding? She was still married?"

"Yep. Her old man wouldn't give her a divorce. Picture an asshole with control issues. She kept thinking she'd get a divorce at any time and then it just became a thing. He showed up a couple of years ago engaged to Jenna, the woman who just left."

Jenna had mentioned her husband and a baby. "Merilee's ex lives here and they just had a kid?"

"Hell, no. Merilee ran his ass out on the rails once she got her paperwork signed." He grinned and nodded his satisfaction with his woman's actions. "Jenna decided to stay. She married a guy she knew from high school last year. Nice fellow. Speaking of marriage and divorce, sorry to hear about Natalie."

"How'd you know about Natalie?"

"Dirk. He rolled in last September, stayed a couple of months and then rolled back out."

Liam's cousin Dirk did that. He'd show up for a while and then vamoose. Dirk was something of a rolling stone. And they'd had some damn good times together as kids and teenagers. Dirk was a year younger than Liam and Lars and a year older than Liam's baby brother, Jack. The four of them had spent many a summer vacation and holidays fishing, hunting, making slingshots, four-wheeling, skinny-dipping, generally doing a bunch of fun stuff at their grandparents' spread in upper Michigan.

And that Dirk would know about his and Natalie's divorce made sense. Liam's mom didn't get along with her two brothers, Bull and Dirk's dad. However, Natalie and Dirk had grown up next door to each other and their moms were good friends. Hell, that's how he'd met Natalie in the first place.

In fact, Natalie had been a sore spot between Liam

and his cousin. Liam hadn't known he was encroaching at the time, and the truth was, it probably wouldn't have made any difference. Dirk thought Liam had stolen Natalie from him, and it had definitely driven a wedge between the two of them.

Liam felt sure that Natalie's mom had been the one to tell of his and Natalie's breakup. You knew you were in a crazy family when your former mother-in-law was the one telling your kin about your divorce.

"How long was Dirk here?" Liam asked. He was sorry he'd missed his cousin. He hadn't seen him in probably six years or more.

"For a couple of months."

Behind him, Tansy stood. He sensed her movement. The mirror beneath the stuffed moose head mounted on the back wall over the bar merely confirmed it.

Unlike nearly every other person in the room, she didn't approach them for an introduction. He looked over his shoulder at her retreating backside as she headed for the door. Bull followed Liam's gaze.

"So, what's her story?" Liam said.

There was no point in anything other than cutting to the chase. Bull would see straight through it.

"She's working on a book. She caught her fiancé fooling around on her and came here to get away for a while and finish up her work. She got here last week and she'll be heading out at the end of the month."

"Ah. One of those scorned women hating on men."

"I wouldn't say that. She strikes me as a nice gal. Now when she asks if you're one of those scorned divorced men hating on women, what should I say?"

"What makes you think she'll ask?"

"Oh, she'll ask. What should I tell her?"

She'd sighted him in her crosshairs. She'd peered down her scope at him. He didn't like it one damn bit. "Tell her it's none of her business."

TANSY STEPPED OUT INTO the September sun and hesitated as the door to Gus's Restaurant and Bar swung shut behind her. Indecision washed through her. She really should just head back to the cabin and get to work. However, focus didn't seem to be her strong suit these days. If she went back out there now without knowing who the stranger with the magnetic gray eyes was, well, she'd simply sit around and wonder.

Jenna was going to be tied up with a client so asking her was out, and the need to know burned inside her.

"What's up, Tansy?"

Lost in her own indecision, she'd missed Alberta's approach. Which merely proved how distracted Tansy had been by the nonverbal encounter with the stranger because Alberta was one hard lady to overlook.

Alberta was, in a word, "colorful." A flowered kerchief covered some of her bright red hair. A brocade vest topped a mutton-sleeved cream blouse. Full, multicolored panels comprised her handkerchief-hemmed skirt, which ended right above her lace-up ankle boots. Turquoise eye shadow, Popsicle-orange lipstick and purple nail polish rounded out her full presentation of the color spectrum. There wasn't a color known to God or man that Alberta wasn't wearing today.

"Not a lot on going on," Tansy said. "I just grabbed a bite to eat with Jenna. How about you?"

"Can't complain." Alberta issued a gap-toothed grin. "Me and Dwight are still in that honeymoon stage."

The thought that she, Tansy, wouldn't have a honeymoon because Bradley was a liar and a cheater, crossed her mind. She brushed it aside, focusing on Alberta and the conversation.

That was the remarkable thing about Good Riddance. Tansy had only been here a week, but between Jenna's weekly emails and being here, she felt fully tuned-in to the town and its people.

Alberta, a traveling Gypsy matchmaker, had shown up in Good Riddance back in May. She'd wound up marrying the man who'd commissioned her to find him a wife.

Dwight Simmons had spent most of his life prospecting and his latter years playing chess and checkers with his prospecting partner, Jeb Taylor. When Jeb died, Dwight decided he was ready for a wife and sought Alberta's expertise. She'd found him one all right—her.

At eighty-one, it was his first marriage. Dwight was Alberta's sixth husband. It was all rather mind-boggling in a charming way.

Actually, Alberta had proven comforting. Within two days of Tansy's arrival, Alberta had corralled her and told Tansy not to worry about Bradley. According to the psychic/matchmaker, Bradley wasn't the one for Tansy and his infidelity was a reflection of him, not her. It was all standard comfort-your-dumped-friend verbiage. Tansy had found some solace in being told she hadn't fallen short as a woman because it was all too easy to feel inadequate when you'd expected to spend your life with a man while he was busy seeking the next best thing.

It was sweet to hear Alberta talk about her new marriage. "A honeymoon stage is good."

"You'd better believe it." A sly wink and an elbow

nudge accompanied her words. "I'm on my way to check in on my stud muffins. Why don't you walk over and say hi with me?"

Dwight and Lord Byron, Alberta's three-legged tom-cat, both hung out at the airstrip center office. Tansy couldn't exactly see either Dwight or Lord Byron as stud-muffin material, but, as with beauty, reality was in the eye of the beholder.

It sounded good to Tansy. She wasn't ready to get back to work and perhaps if she knew who the stranger was, she could shake off the impact of those few seconds when his eyes had pierced hers. And the surest source of information was Merilee.

Tansy trailed along with Alberta to the door halfway down the front of the building.

They stepped into the airstrip office, the scent of cookies and coffee in the air. Merilee and one of the bush pilots, a pretty, newly married brunette named Juliette, had their heads together over paperwork at Merilee's desk. Juliette and her husband, Sven, were her neighbors out at Shadow Lake. Juliette's husky puppy, Baby, sat waiting patiently between the two women. Baby actually flew in the plane with Juliette on trips. It was cute.

The object of Alberta's affections sat across the room, staring at the chess table before him. Dwight not only had a new wife, but a new chess partner had materialized in Jefferson Walker Monroe.

According to Jenna, Jefferson had simply walked into town one day and sat down in the rocking chair on the other side of the chess set and that had been that. It turned out that the only relative Jefferson had left was Curl, the town's taxidermist, mortician and barber.

Curl hadn't actually known he had a long-lost relative, particularly a man of color who recounted stories of playing the saxophone with greats such as Count Basie and Louis Armstrong and playing studio sessions with Billie Holiday and Ella Fitzgerald. However, Curl had embraced Jefferson, as had the rest of the town's people.

Tansy had looked him up on Google. Jefferson Walker Monroe was the real deal.

In so many ways, Good Riddance was like the collection of Santa's misfit toys from the Rudolph the Red-nosed Reindeer TV classic. Maybe that's why Tansy felt right at home.

Dwight and Jefferson sat on opposite sides of the chessboard. They were a study in juxtaposition, their only commonalities white hair and lined faces. Both men had witnessed the change of seasons for more than eight decades.

Dwight's long white beard and fringe of white hair rested against the collar of his checked flannel shirt. Long summer days and harsh winters had weathered his skin to a permanent ruddiness. Tall and thin, his carriage bore a permanent stoop. His overalls, while clean, were as worn and weathered as his face.

Across the table, Jefferson bespoke a sophistication of a bygone era of well-dressed couples, two-olive martinis and a husky-voiced chanteuse in evening wear. With his close-cropped white hair, wire-rimmed spectacles and well-pressed suit he should've appeared ridiculous in a town ruled by work boots and flannel. However, he simply looked like a man comfortable in his own skin, waiting to be called onstage to play the next set.

Lord Byron, who was possibly the ugliest cat Tansy had ever seen, but had survivor written all over him, lay curled on top of the empty potbellied stove.

"Hey, sweet thing," Alberta said loudly to Dwight, whose hearing wasn't so good these days.

The cat's ears pricked but he didn't open his eyes.

Before Dwight could respond, Jefferson smiled, mischief glinting in his eyes. "I've told you not to talk to me that way in front of your old man."

"Hey, beautiful," Dwight said to his wife. Most assuredly a case of beauty in the eye of the beholder. He turned back to his chess partner. "Don't make me call you out, talking to my wife that way."

"Won't make any difference if you're not any better at fighting than you are at chess. And if you don't have better moves behind closed doors than you do on the chessboard...."

Dwight grumbled beneath his breath and moved a chess piece.

Tansy laughed at the byplay as Merilee looked over her shoulder. "Afternoon, ladies."

Tansy waved. Alberta spoke up. "What's shaking, Merilee? Juliette?"

Juliette opened the back door. "I'm off to Wolf Pass for a pickup. See you guys later." Baby trotted out behind her.

Merilee stood, stretching. "Bull's nephew Liam just got into town. We haven't seen him in years. We knew he was coming but we just didn't know when." Merilee looked at Tansy, a question in her eyes. "He was just over at Gus's."

Liam. Tansy turned the name over in her head. It fit. It was unusual, and the man himself, in that brief

moment of eye contact, had struck her as just that—
unusual.

"I saw someone with Bull, but there are still people
in town that I don't know. Or rather who live out of
town." There were a number of people, men mostly, who
lived out in the wilderness surrounding Good Riddance.

"Liam's a nice name," Alberta said.

Merilee nodded. "He's a nice guy. We don't know
the whole story but he just got out of the Marines. He
was a sharpshooter. I'm surprised he's out—don't know
why—but I'm glad he's here."

Something slid over Tansy. A sharpshooter. The
man's sole purpose had been to kill people. Hard. Dangerous.

"When did he get out of the military?" Alberta said.

Merilee shrugged. "All we know is Bull got an email
from his sister saying he left in May setting out for here.
His sister's not the most reliable source. We thought for
years Liam and Lars had joined the Army. Where he's
been in between or what happened, I have no idea."

"So, I guess he's not married or he wouldn't have
left his wife behind?" Alberta pursed her lips in con-
sideration.

"He's divorced. His cousin Dirk told us when he was
here. Liam's got a twin, Lars, who's also a Marine and
a younger brother, Jack, who's a Navy SEAL, but beyond that—" another shrug from Merilee "—is a mystery. Bull and his sister have been estranged for several
years now. She's an odd bird and doesn't seem to play
well with others."

None of it should matter to Tansy any more than
any of the other people she'd encountered here, but
strangely it did. There was something about the man

that attracted her, drew her, from the moment she exchanged that glance. She felt unsettled inside…well, even more so than before. And it wasn't just a curiosity. It was a sexual attraction, a wanting that had been instant, and it was a feeling that she simply wasn't accustomed to. She'd felt desire with Bradley, but that had been a culmination of getting to know him, of wooing and bonding that grew as she got to know who Bradley was inside. Although she'd obviously been way off the mark with what was inside Bradley. How could she have been so wrong about him? She wanted to just wake up and have things the way they used to be. However, she kept those thoughts to herself, not even sharing them with Jenna.

But how could she be attracted to a stranger when she still felt that way about Bradley?

"Interesting," Alberta said, and for one disconcerting moment Tansy thought the other woman was commenting on what had been rolling through Tansy's head. But then she realized Alberta was merely commenting on Merilee's rundown on Liam. "Where's he gonna stay?" Alberta said.

"Bull and I have talked about it and discussed it with Skye and Dalton. We knew he was coming, just not when. He's going to stay in the other cabin out at Shadow Lake." Merilee smiled at Tansy. "Liam's your new neighbor."

MALLORY KINCAID GNAWED on the end of her pen—a bad habit, that—as she stared at the blinking cursor on her computer screen. The air conditioner hummed in the background, working overtime in the humid heat of Louisiana's Indian summer. She could close the blind on the hot sun slanting through the window but she liked the feel of it against her skin.

Good Riddance, Alaska. The satellite image showed a small town, with one main street running through its center and surrounded by trees. Lots and lots of trees.

That's where Liam Reinhardt was now. She quit gnawing on the pen and placed it on top of one of the piles on her desk. He obviously wasn't trying to hide. It'd been easy to follow him via his credit card usage.

He'd left Minnesota and headed southwest, rolling through South Dakota, Wyoming, Idaho, back north into Montana, west again to Washington and finally Alaska via Canada. He hadn't been in any hurry. He'd spent four months traveling, alternating between motels and campgrounds.

He might pick up and move on tomorrow, but Mallory had a feeling he'd finally arrived at his destination. His uncle lived in Good Riddance. Bull Swenson owned a hardware store/sawmill and the deed to several parcels of land in addition to an interest in the airstrip and the local eatery—public records were a beautiful thing.

The remoteness of the Alaskan wilderness seemed to fit Liam Reinhardt perfectly. She just couldn't imagine a man like him settling down in the suburbs.

It'd been a crapshoot when he was discharged. She figured he'd either land at Quantico as a civilian adviser or he'd go to ground. Apparently he was going to ground.

She opened another tab and typed in flight information. She winced at the results. She hadn't thought it would be cheap, but it was going to be damn expensive to get herself there. However, she had to do what she had to do. A couple of keystrokes later and she was printing her boarding pass for a flight tomorrow.

And that was the easy part. Adrenaline surged through her. The challenge lay in getting Liam Reinhardt to actually talk to her. And part of that adrenaline surge was due to the fact that she was admittedly infatuated with and fascinated by the man.

She came from a military family and had pursued a career as a military historian. She'd grown up surrounded by men in uniform and had always considered them a cut above the rest, but there were always a handful of men who stood out even above them. Liam Reinhardt was one of those men.

He'd performed brilliantly in what was his final mission. It hadn't gotten a lot of coverage in the media, which was the way the corps had wanted it, but those with military knowledge knew the importance of what had gone down, and that Reinhardt had been the one to deliver the goods. She had seen him a year ago in a video conference when she'd been in a Marine general's office on a documenting assignment and had been smitten from the moment she'd seen him and heard his voice—online, that is. Since then she'd followed his career, researched him and come to realize he was the man meant for her.

She glanced at his framed picture sitting on her desk. Those eyes, the hard glint of his stare, the line of his jaw. She smiled and reached over and traced her finger against the glass that separated her from his image. She'd found it of him in military files and had the photo printed. There was also one sitting on her nightstand.

He was only one of the best sharpshooters in military history, right up there with legendary sharpshooter

Carlos Hathcock of Vietnam-era fame. He was precisely
what she'd always dreamed of in a man. Handsome yet
rugged, highly accomplished and self-contained—how
could a woman not be in love with a man like that?

While getting him to share the story of his last mission with her might be a challenge, she knew that once
they met he'd recognize her as his fate, as surely as she
knew he was hers.

As mere mortals neither of them could deny a force
stronger than them—destiny.

They were meant to be together.

3

"GOT ANY PLANS?" Bull asked as they stepped outside. A truck with more rust than actual body parts passed and Bull automatically waved. It was that kind of town.

"Thought I'd just chill for a while." The words almost stuck in his throat. He had no purpose. He was rudderless. He was well acquainted with stillness and quietness of being—it had been vital to his job. This was different. He'd be damned if he knew what to do with himself.

Bull nodded. "Think you might be interested in some seasonal construction work? Sven Sorenson can always use an extra set of hands, and he's up to his eyeballs in work these days."

"Is it hard labor?"

"It can be."

"Then count me in." He needed to work himself into exhaustion. Maybe then he could actually sleep at night.

The airstrip/bed-and-breakfast door opened and the woman from the booth, the woman who'd seemed to sink into him—Tansy—stepped out onto the sidewalk.

"See you later," she called over her shoulder, closing the door behind her.

Both Bull and Liam stopped, but the sun must have been in her eyes, because she walked right into Liam. Instinctively he grabbed her to deflect the impact.

Every sense inside him went on high alert, which translated to everything slowing down to utter awareness. The wind from the northeast carried her scent of woman—vanilla and a hint of spice. Her skin was soft and warm beneath his hands, her flesh firm to his touch. Her eyes, somewhere between blue and almost purple, widened behind her glasses in surprise and a flash of recognition.

Something wild and hot sprang between them. Liam wasn't used to wild and hot. It wasn't his modus operandi. He did only a controlled heat. Her eyes widened even more and he felt a tremor chase through her. She recognized it as well, and he fully suspected it was outside her normal range, too.

He released her.

She dropped her gaze.

"Thank you."

Her voice, low, husky and damned sexy resonated through him. What the hell was wrong with him? What was it with this woman?

"Steady there," Bull said from his side, ending his loss of composure. He'd totally forgotten Bull was even there. Crap. "Tansy, meet Liam Reinhardt, my nephew. Liam, this is Tansy Wellington."

"Nice to meet you," he said automatically. He didn't offer his hand and neither did she. It seemed unnecessary, considering they'd already touched. And because he wanted so badly to touch her again, he wouldn't.

"It's nice to meet you, too." There was a softness to her that made him want to taste her. The thought crossed his mind that her honeyed sweetness might mitigate some of the bitterness and anger inside him. He pushed aside the notion. "I hear you just got into town," he said.

She smiled and it knocked him for yet another loop, lighting her face and transforming her from ordinary to extraordinary in the blink of an eye. "I just arrived last week. I'm not one of the regulars."

"So I hear."

"You'll both find," Bull said, "that news travels faster than the speed of light here."

Her laugh held the same husky sexiness that made him think of lying in bed with her, both of them naked. That and the way her T-shirt clung to the roundness of her breasts and followed the curve of her waist to her full hips.

"I understand we're going to be neighbors," she said.

What the hell? "We are?" Liam looked to Bull.

"Janie—" God, his mother hated that name, preferring the more formal Jane "—gave us the heads-up you were heading this way. Me and Merilee figured you'd want a little privacy, so we made arrangements for you to stay in one of the cabins at Shadow Lake, outside of town. Tansy's staying in the other cabin." Bull looked at Tansy. "Nice place, isn't it?"

She nodded. "It's beautiful. The cabins overlook a lake surrounded by mountains."

He could almost feel her encroaching on him. She painted a scene of tranquillity at odds with the seething inside him. He wanted solitude to embrace his anger, not dispel it. He didn't want to be seduced by her dulcet tones, her ripeness, her sweetness. He wanted distance from her. "How many cabins are there?" he said to Bull, knowing damn well he was bordering on rude.

"Only the two. They belonged to two old maids who built them next to one another. They're within spitting distance. There's even a crude intercom system that was left in place. Sven just overhauled them a couple of months ago. They're nice enough, but not fussy. It should suit your needs."

How the hell would Bull know what his needs were when he wasn't even sure of them? All he knew was that he needed to be alone and he needed time. But how could he be alone, with this woman right next door?

As if he'd gained some inside track on what was going through Liam's head, Bull added, "Trust me on this."

If there was anyone in this world, other than his twin, whom he trusted, it was Bull Swenson. He looked at Tansy Wellington standing there in the sunshine.

He was in trouble....

TANSY SETTLED IN on the couch with her laptop. A small desk sat against one wall, but she preferred propping her feet on the coffee table and working from there. It wasn't exactly balmy outside. She'd thrown on a cardigan over her T-shirt and would start up the potbellied stove in a bit. She loved the smell of wood smoke against the crispness of the autumn evenings here. For now, the front door stood open, with the screen door guarding against bugs and anything that might wander up.

She would get to work. She would power through this. Five minutes later she'd gotten a big fat nowhere. And now instead of Bradley burning into her brain, she had both Bradley and Liam occupying that space. Actually, Liam was pushing Bradley to the background.

She sighed, frustrated with herself, and set aside her laptop. Wrapping her sweater around her, she walked out to the front porch and sat on the bottom step, soaking up the sun. It glinted off the lake's surface. Snow capped the mountains that stood as a backdrop. They appeared close enough to touch, but were actually quite a distance away. It was tranquillity incarnate. She sighed again and leaned her head against the porch post.

She didn't want this man in the cabin next door. And it *was* right next door. He was hard and wounded…and she was attracted to him. The feel of his hard palms against her had set off an unwelcome need to have more. She'd been relieved, yet disappointed, when he'd dropped his hands from her arms.

The roar of a motorcycle approaching disturbed the quiet. It was him. She didn't know that he drove a motorcycle, but it fit. She heard the downshift as he turned onto the driveway from the main road. She forced herself not to get up and go inside. She would not run, scurrying inside like some frightened little mouse, despite the temptation to do just that.

He emerged from the stand of trees on a black beast of a motorcycle. She openly watched his approach. It would be silly to pretend she didn't see or hear him.

He, however, ignored her as he drove past to park in front of the cabin next to hers. He killed the engine and climbed off. He was tall and lean, yet broad shouldered, and she'd have to be dead not to notice that he had a nice derriere in those jeans. She most assuredly wasn't dead.

He pulled off his helmet and without hesitation

crossed the expanse separating them. She thought about remaining seated, but that would put his crotch directly at eye level, which didn't seem the best idea.

She rose and tamped down the urge to wrap her arms around her middle. He was intimidating in his black leather jacket. Actually, it wasn't even the jacket. It was the attitude. She, however, refused to be intimidated.

He cut to the chase. "I came here for privacy."

What the heck? "So did I."

"I don't want a neighbor."

For a moment his sheer nerve and arrogance rendered her speechless. And then that moment passed. "News flash, Captain Sharpshooter—"

"That's Sergeant Sharpshooter."

Whatever. "You didn't corner that market. I came here for privacy and I don't want a neighbor, either. And if I did, it sure as heck wouldn't be you. However, churlishness isn't in my nature, so I will make the best of what has become a bad situation."

"Really?" He crossed his arms over his chest, and she had the distinct impression, despite his dour expression, that she was amusing him. "So how do you plan to make the best of what you term a bad situation? Are you going to move in with your sister?"

"Hardly. If anyone were to seek alternative arrangements, that would be you. I was here first. So are you going to move in with your aunt and uncle?"

"Nope. I told you I want privacy."

"Have I invaded your privacy? I was sitting here minding my own business and you walked over to my cabin."

"I wanted to make my position clear."

"It's crystal clear. And I hope you're not suffering any confusion as to where I stand, either."

"I don't want any company or milk and cookies or any of that neighborly crap."

"I don't bake, so no worries. And if I was seeking out company, it certainly wouldn't be yours."

"Same here, sister."

She wasn't sure whether she wanted to cry or throw something at him. Both were atypical behavior and neither was a viable option.

"Good," she said.

"Great."

"Better than great." By God, she'd have the last word with this moron.

"By the way, I don't plan to alter the way I do things on your behalf."

Merilee was seriously confused if she thought Liam was a nice guy. He was a jerk. "I don't recall asking you to." And then curiosity got the best of her. "Like what exactly? Should I expect you to howl at the moon?"

"I only howl occasionally, but I do swim in the nude."

He swam in the nude? She didn't know whether he was just trying to shock her or if he was serious. Either way, she felt her face heating with a blush. Nonetheless, she called his bluff. "Yet another news flash, Sergeant." She looked around as if checking that no one else was nearby and lowered her voice to a conspiratorial whisper. "I've seen nude men before. I think I'll manage to contain myself."

"I just don't need a jilted man-hating woman taking out her frustrations on me."

Really? Seriously? That had just come out of his mouth? *Jerk* didn't begin to describe him. She gathered every ounce of self-control and smiled sweetly at him. "I am shocked, simply shocked, that you're not married. Such gallantry and charm—you're such a catch it's unfathomable you arrived alone. It will require great willpower on my part, but I think I can manage to not show up on your doorstep, craving your fun-loving, witty company, or throw myself at your nakedness when you go for your swim."

His expression remained implacable. "I think we've come to an understanding." He turned to go.

Almost. "One more thing, Sergeant…"

He gave a quarter turn to face her again. "Yes?"

"I don't know, and quite frankly I don't care, what your problem is, but you need to find another whipping post. Stay the hell away from me."

SON OF A BITCH. That tactic had failed miserably. Well, it hadn't been a total wash from the standpoint that she'd certainly give him a wide berth now, but it hadn't sent her packing, which had been the overall plan. She was still within spitting distance.

He'd underestimated her.

There was a tactic that when a soldier found himself outmanned and alone, he pulled out all his weapons and went on the offensive, guns blazing. He might get gunned down, regardless, but odds were the enemy would turn and flee, sure that anyone on such a certain attack had reinforcements behind him. Liam had dubbed it "playing crazy." He supposed he'd dub what he'd just done "playing super-bastard." He'd gone on the offensive and been incredibly abrasive and rude.

He'd fully expected her to turn tail and run. He'd counted on her to quail and take cover by moving into town, away from him. Instead, she'd not only stood her ground, but returned fire, volley for volley.

She was a worthy adversary.

He found himself whistling as he emptied his backpack and stored his meager provisions.

The cabin was comfortable, just the other side of utilitarian. He preferred no frills, and this place provided just that. He immediately noted the entrances and exits—one door in the front, one in the back on the other side of the kitchen.

A single room accommodated a kitchen and sofa with a small desk. A television sat against the opposite wall. The two other rooms were a bathroom and a bedroom. The bathroom held a double bed, small dresser, nightstand and standing wardrobe for clothes. A large braided rug covered a good portion of the wood floor in the main room, with a smaller version of the same color and design in the bedroom.

Framed nature prints hung on the walls. An eagle at roost. A pair of loons on the water. The unblinking stare of a bull moose. Some purple flowers. Spruce hanging heavy with snow.

Nice.

Bull had contacted Sven Sorenson, who had stopped by to meet Liam. Liam would start working with Sven's crew tomorrow. He'd asked for the most physically demanding job Sven could throw his way.

Liam craved a workout. He ran every morning, but it wasn't enough—he needed to push himself to the point of physical exhaustion. The sun seemed to wink off the water in invitation. Liam had met the other two couples who lived here—Skye and Dalton Saunders and Sven and Juliette Sorenson. They were all at work.

Liam was going for a swim. It was brisk, but he'd swam in much colder water. As boys in Wisconsin, he and his brother had always swam in the altogether when they could get away with it. Maybe this would send her packing.

He tugged off his boots and socks and stepped outside, clad only in his T-shirt, jeans and underwear. The grass was soft beneath his feet. It had been a long time since he'd walked barefoot on a carpet of green like this.

The water would be cold. That was fine. He'd embrace the cold, adapt to it, push through it.

The hair on the back of his neck prickled to attention. She was there. He felt her watching him. Dammit—he wanted to her *gone*. Methodically, without fanfare, he stripped.

He waded in, the bracingly cold water lapping around him, and he kept going. Once he hit waist-deep, he began to swim. He focused on the strokes, the rhythm, mentally calculating his distance until the physicality of it freed his mind.

TANSY STOOD ROOTED to her spot behind the screen door, mesmerized by the sheer beauty of the man moving through the water.

The water rippled about him as his powerful strokes cut through the surface. Muscles rippled along his arms, shoulders and back. The effect rippled through her.

He'd disturbed her surface. He'd broken her calm… well, what little calm she'd had. He'd shattered it in spades.

Watching him strip on the shoreline—and yeah, she'd watched—had been something else. Yes, she'd seen a naked man before…and Bradley hadn't looked like that. Hard and muscled, Liam's body bespoke discipline and rigor. She had no doubt that whatever physical demands he encountered, he was up to the task. He didn't have the bulk and bulge of a weight lifter, but sleek, honed definition. The man didn't carry an ounce of fat and if she'd thought his derriere was impressive in jeans, it had been beyond compare in the altogether.

She'd called his bluff and he'd delivered.

He'd told her he would do what he would do and wouldn't change anything up for her. And he had.

She opened the screen door and stepped out onto the porch, into the waning sunlight. Leaning against the post, she openly watched him. If an unattractive, albeit boorish, man chose to strip naked and swim in the lake in front of her temporary home, then she chose to watch. Plus, she was curious as to just how far and long he'd swim.

Another plus in the equation was it really was rather akin to poetry in motion to watch his movements in the water. Fluid and powerful, he seemed at one with the lake. And last but not least, given how impressive the rear view had been, she readily admitted she wanted to see how the front view stacked up.

There was something about that argument and then subsequently watching him disrobe that had only heightened the sexual attraction she'd felt from the instant she'd seen him. And in a way, she had enjoyed that blowup. She'd welcomed the anger and outrage. He'd been a distraction and an outlet. For the entire time she'd been arguing with him, she hadn't thought of Bradley, not in any portion of her brain, except when the butthead had mentioned her being jilted or whatever nonsense he'd said. But then she really still hadn't thought of Bradley—it had been more about her.

And it had been good to feel something more—even if it was anger and outrage…and this sexual tingling—than the numbness that had permeated her since she'd walked away from Bradley and his infidelity.

Lost in her own musings, she realized his pace had slowed. A few yards from the shore, he stopped swimming and stood. Her breath caught in her throat and her heart rate accelerated as he began to walk to the water's edge. Wet, dark hair was scattered over his chest, a taut belly and then—oh…my…goodness. She swallowed hard, a white-hot heat arcing from her brain straight to her sex. Sweet mercy. It was chilly, the water was cold… and he was still impressive. Certainly more impressive than what she'd seen in her other views of male nudity. What he hadn't been gifted with in the way of manners he'd been given in physical endowments because…well, wow. He was a jerk, but a well-hung jerk.

Maybe that was part of his problem—too much testosterone. She'd always favored gentle, academic men who tended to be a little on the soft side. There was nothing gentle, academic or soft about the naked man retrieving his clothes from the ground.

He straightened and she wasn't surprised at all that he made absolutely no attempt to cover his nakedness. She made absolutely no attempt to avert her eyes.

He strode audaciously, surely, toward his cabin. She watched boldly, the play of muscles in his thighs, the weight of his penis between his legs, the slide of water over his golden skin.

Neither of them spoke a word. He stared straight ahead. She stared straight at him, silently challenging him to say something to acknowledge her presence when he'd vowed to ignore her.

Actually, he didn't have to speak to acknowledge her. Awareness arced between them; sexual tension fairly sizzled in the air.

Insanely, if he detoured and his path led him naked to her, despite his earlier behavior she wouldn't turn away. She fairly hummed with a newfound sexual energy…that suddenly needed an outlet.

But he didn't detour and come to stand before her. He went inside his cabin and closed the door behind him.

She sank to the top step, feeling both weak-kneed and energized at the same time. She felt alive and turned on.

He wanted a war? She'd give him a war.

Tansy smiled to herself and reached into her pocket for her cell phone.

She knew just the next move.

4

LIAM TURNED OUT THE LIGHT and stretched out on the bed, his hands folded beneath his head. Why the hell did everything have to be so damn complicated?

All he'd wanted was a military career, and that was gone. It'd been easy not to think about Natalie and her leaving him when he'd had his job to fill his mind. His job had always come first. Now his failed marriage was horning into his thoughts.

There was the woman next door. And he'd gotten an email from Lars. His twin had leave coming up and was heading to Good Riddance.

He pushed up off of the bed and crossed to the window. It wasn't exactly hot but he'd spent so much time bunking down in tents and out in the field that he slept better with a little fresh air circulating around him. He raised the blind and opened the window a couple of inches. Cool night air seeped into the room and a slice of star-scattered sky was visible with the blinds raised.

He settled back on the bed, his hands once again folded beneath his head. Peripheral movement caught his eye. Next door, the lights had gone out in the main part of the cabin. Seconds later the lamp switched on in the bedroom. With the light on and the blinds down, she was like a shadow puppet as she moved about the room.

And then she really caught and held his attention when she, in outline, tugged the T-shirt over her head. The woman had a classic hourglass figure. She was built the way women were supposed to be built, with curves and a little extra padding here and there.

He rolled to his side and watched while she slid her jeans over her hips. Turning one-hundred eighty degrees, she reached behind her and unhooked her bra. She stood there for a moment, outlined in cock-hardening relief, the fullness of her breast, the slight sag that said they were real and the thrusts of her nipples all clearly detailed in the play of shadow.

She slipped her panties off and there was the curve of her belly and ass, the faint unevenness of pubic hair. He lay transfixed, his breathing growing as heavy as his cock, when she lightly ran her hands over her breasts, palming the points. Then she slid one hand down her belly and dipped her fingers between her thighs and he could almost feel the moisture gathered there, smell the scent of her arousal in the air.

She sank to the bed and extinguished the light but he knew what she was doing and as surely as he knew triangulation, he knew that she'd been turned on by him. She wasn't thinking about whatever Joe Blow she'd been engaged to. When she'd touched herself, Liam had been the man in mind.

And it was hot to know she was next door thinking of him while she fingered herself. She was hot. It had been a while since he'd been with a woman and he wanted her. He closed his eyes as he wrapped his hand around his cock. He didn't think he'd ever been this horny. He let his mind drift....

Her eyes glittering the way they had earlier in the day, she lowered her head to his waiting penis. She dragged her wet tongue up one side and down the other, then she took him into the wet warmth of her mouth and sucked on him. Her mouth felt so good wrapped around him. He was damn near at the point of exploding. He dragged her off of his cock and flipped her to her back, lapping at her tight, taut nipples, suckling her while he filled his hands with her soft, full breasts. He couldn't wait...couldn't hold back... He nudged the head of his dick against her, coating himself with her slick juices and then buried himself deep inside her tight channel... again...and again...and again until he unloaded deep inside her while she spasmed around him, milking him with her orgasm.

Spent, he lay there, his breathing heavy and ragged.

And in his fevered brain, in the quiet of the night, he could've sworn he heard the faint echoes of her own cries as she found her release.

THE NEXT MORNING TANSY stood in her T-shirt and panties, scrambling eggs at the stove. She'd had the best night's rest since she'd been here. Masturbation didn't even come close to a man's touch, the slide of skin against skin, the fullness of a man's penis inside her, but her orgasm as she'd imagined hard, rough sex—which was unlike any sex she'd had before—with Sergeant Alpha-Male Sharpshooter next door had been great. She'd slept like a baby and woken up ravenous.

The screen door slammed and she glanced out the window. Liam wore running shoes, shorts and a sweat-shirt. The man boasted some nice legs, that was for sure. She'd sort of missed that yesterday, she'd been so busy checking out other parts of his anatomy. Nicely muscled. He was just altogether a fine specimen of a man.

He took off at a jog on the trail to the left of the cabins that skirted the lake. Swimming. Running. It all explained that nice hard body. With a start she realized she was scorching her eggs. She yanked the pan off the burner. His arrogant self would probably love the fact that she'd nearly burned her breakfast because of him.

Regardless, she ate the eggs, at least the ones that hadn't stuck to the bottom of the pan, and headed into the bedroom to get dressed. She eyed her meager wardrobe, hesitating in a way she never did over what to wear. Defiantly, she pulled on her least favorite shirt she'd packed and a pair of jeans. She might be in some crazy heightened sexual state over the man next door but she'd be damned if she'd alter her routine because of him.

Ten minutes later, face washed, teeth and hair brushed, minimal makeup on, she settled on the sofa with her laptop. She opened her document and got herself oriented in the work.

Engrossed, she heard the motorcycle roar to life. She glanced at her clock. She'd been at it for an hour and a half. And she'd accomplished more today than she had since her arrival last week. She supposed she should've tried a head-to-head argument and masturbation earlier. Infuriating man.

With a grin, she got back to work, the sound of the motorcycle fading in the distance.

Midmorning, she'd just stood to stretch when the truck rumbled down the driveway. She went out onto the front porch. The driver, an older man with salt-and-pepper hair and beard, rolled down the window. "Name's Clyde. Bull sent me."

"Hi, I'm Tansy. If you could just put it right there." She pointed to the area separating the two cabins.

Clyde climbed out of the cab. He picked up the first bag of sand out of the cargo bed. "You want me to spread it around or something?"

"No. You can just put them there."

She'd called Bull yesterday to see if he stocked sand and some rope. She was in luck on both counts. She'd planned to drive in but he'd offered to have Clyde stop by with it on his way to deliver supplies to Sven's crew. It worked for her.

"Whatever you say." He stacked the bags where she'd indicated and added the length of rope she'd also ordered. "So, you making some kind of beach or something here?"

His look clearly said he thought she'd lost her mind. She wasn't too sure that she hadn't. Her plan was a little out there. It might have to do with being in Alaska, or at this cabin, or maybe it was her experience with Bradley, or even something to do with Liam that had sparked something in her. On the other hand, like the last box on a multiple choice test, it might be all of the above. Whatever the reason, the idea had just popped into her head, and although she normally would've dismissed it, she was going with it.

"Not a beach. Just something."

"Alrighty then. Bull said to leave the shovel, as well, so here ya go."

"Thanks so much." Tansy tried to press a five-dollar tip into Clyde's hand.

"Sorry, can't take that. Bull wouldn't like it."

"Tell him I said thank you so much and I really appreciate it." Clyde was heading out to the construction site where Liam was working. "Oh, yeah, and remember not to say anything because this is a surprise for Sergeant Reinhardt."

Clyde grinned, obviously delighted to be part of a surprise, even if he did think she was nuts. "My lips are sealed."

An hour later, Tansy's shoulders ached and she'd worked up a sweat. Stepping back, she eyed her handiwork.

Perfect. Absolutely perfect.

"YOU DO GOOD WORK," Sven Sorenson said.

Liam had spent the day carrying and hanging Sheetrock. They were building a bed-and-breakfast on the outskirts of town. They'd all headed over to Gus's for some lunch and while the place had been crowded and he'd seen Jenna, Tansy hadn't been there. Sven's crew, however, was a good group of guys.

"Thanks." Liam liked the big blond guy who could've doubled as a Viking stand-in in an action flick. "So do you." Sven had remodeled/updated the cabins out at Shadow Lake.

The other man smiled. "I try. So, same time tomorrow? I can use you if you're up for it."

"I'll be here." Liam nodded and walked over to his motorcycle. A few minutes later he was opening the throttle on his bike, relaxing into the ride. It had been hard work, but it hadn't pushed him to his limit, not even with the run he'd gotten in ahead of time.

He drove along the road that had been cut through

the towering evergreens. Clouds dotted the expanse of blue sky. The wind felt good against his skin. It was one of the best days he'd had since he'd been told about his discharge. It was good to be in the company of men all working toward a common purpose, even if it wasn't defeating the enemy.

Tansy had drifted through his thoughts throughout the day. Her front door had been closed when he went out for his run this morning and it had still been shut when he'd headed out to work. But she'd been there and she'd been up. He'd sensed her, felt her looking at him when he'd set out on his morning run, the way he'd always felt a countersniper sighting him.

He turned onto the road leading to the cabins and there she was, sitting on the front step, the same as she'd been yesterday when he'd arrived. A part of him had wondered if she might have left, but the greater part of him had known she'd still be around.

The late-afternoon sun glinted in her hair, picking up threads of red. She wore jeans and a striped T-shirt, but the clothes really didn't matter because now he knew exactly what curves lay beneath her attire. All that was left was to fill in the details...and he'd more than like to fill in those blanks in his mind. The desire he'd felt yesterday and last night had been simmering beneath his surface all day and now seeing her was like throwing gasoline on an ember—it exploded inside him.

Caught up in her, he didn't notice it until he was almost upon it. What the...? He wanted to throw his head back and laugh. The woman was crazy, mad as a hatter. It was the same kind of crazy tactic he'd employed last night.

He pulled up in front of his cabin, killed the engine

and climbed off. Pulling off his helmet, he walked over to the strip of sand that ran the length of the cabins with a length of rope down the center of the sand. General Wellington, he quickly designated her, had literally drawn a line in the sand.

"And what's this supposed to be?" he said, walking forward until the toe of his boot rested against the rope.

She approached on her side until mere inches, and the line, separated them. She brimmed with smug self-satisfaction…and sexuality. "You're a smart man. I'm sure you know exactly what it is."

God, she smelled good, like sunshine, woman and some bath stuff. Her lips were as full and ripe as the rest of her. He ached to kiss that smirk right off of her face, but that didn't seem to be the best tactical move right now. "So what happens if one of us crosses the line?" he asked in a low tone.

A slight breeze ruffled her hair. The exchange took on a whole new meaning. The shift wasn't lost on her, either. Her eyes widened behind her glasses and the air between them sizzled.

She rimmed her lower lip with the tip of her tongue, a nervous gesture, but it immediately brought to mind his fantasy last night of her mouth on his cock. Her proximity and that memory had an instant hardening effect on him.

"Crossing the line is a very bad idea. Just know there will be dire consequences."

He smiled. Smiling in the face of an enemy messed with its mind. "Is that a fact? I've faced dire consequences before and lived to tell it."

"Clearly," she countered. "Do you always state the obvious?"

"Only to reinforce a point." He inched his boot forward until it rested on the line, nearly over. "What are you going to do about it, Wellington? Or should I call you General Wellington?"

She arched one eyebrow? "Really? You consider this your Waterloo? And if I'm General Wellington, that puts you on the losing side, doesn't it?"

Ha. So, she'd paid attention during world history classes. "What are you prepared to do if I invade your territory?"

"You're the one who made such an issue of your privacy. So, why are you standing here now when we agreed to stay out of each other's business? To ignore each other?"

Jesus, he wanted to touch her, taste her, bury himself in her.

"You're avoiding the question. You drew the line. You never draw the line if you're not willing to back it up with action."

"Don't try me, Reinhardt." He'd never wanted to try a woman more, try her on for size, texture, fit. "It's not a dare. It's just the boundaries you made such a big deal about."

"What are you afraid of?"

"I'm not afraid."

"I call bullshit on that because you can't handle me."

"Maybe I can and maybe I can't, but I can promise you I'll go down trying." I'll go down…her warm wet mouth encompassing him… Dammit, he was throbbing for her. "Just watch me if you—"

"Watching you was a pleasure."

For a second she froze. "You…when…"

He leaned down until her hair brushed against his

face, his lips nearly touching the shell of her ear. "Last night. You were outlined against the blinds. How was it?"

"Oh, God."

"Did you think about me?" He paused and while it might seem for effect, he had to struggle to collect himself. He was far from immune to her nearness. She tested his mettle, his self-control. "I thought about you."

"You…you're reprehensible." But there was no venom behind it, merely a breathless desperation.

"And it doesn't matter, does it, Tansy, because I turn you on, just like you turn me on."

"You don't…" She petered out. "I don't like you."

He respected the fact she didn't deny he turned her on. That took some guts. Wellington was no wimp beneath her soft facade.

"I know. I don't want you to like me."

"Why not? What are you afraid of? What are you so angry about?"

"My business is none of your business."

She stood her ground. "Then don't make it my business." She looked down at where his boot rested on the orange mark. "I'd suggest you continue to toe the line and leave it at that."

Smart-ass. And then he did laugh. "I'll outmaneuver you every time, Wellington."

"It doesn't matter—" she paused deliberately "—Reinhardt. I outrank you. You're just a sergeant—" her grin socked him in the gut "—I'm a general. You're out of your league."

She turned on her heel and walked back to her cabin. He let her go. It wasn't a retreat, but rather a triumphant march. He stood there until the door closed behind her.

Outranked? Perhaps. Out of his league? Never. He'd felled an opposing general with a single shot from a mile away.

General Wellington should be quaking in her proverbial boots.

MALLORY SET HER TRAVEL case at the foot of the quilt-covered double bed in the Good Riddance Bed & Breakfast, which was located on the second floor of the airstrip office.

"Come on down when you get settled and let me know if there's anything you need," Merilee Swenson said.

"Will do. I'm just going to freshen up a bit. It's been a long day."

"Traveling all the way from Louisiana will do that." She shook her head, smiling. "That was some timing that you called just after we got that cancellation. We're at full capacity." She laughed. "All four rooms." She crossed the threshold. "See you in a bit and holler if you need anything." She closed the door behind her.

Mallory sat on the bed's edge and reoriented herself. It had been an exhausting, yet invigorating, day—airports and connections and then the bush plane flight out to here. She'd never been to Alaska before and all the Google images and pictures couldn't begin to do justice to the breathtaking splendor of the Alaskan wilderness.

And she was one step closer to initiating contact with Liam Reinhardt. He hadn't moved on, but then again she'd been sure he wouldn't. He was still here. And in a town this size and given they were both newcomers, an introduction was inevitable. For all she knew, he could be staying in the room next door. And she took it as a providential sign that a room had opened up just before she called.

There had been so many signs that had made the rightness of her and Liam impossible to ignore. She'd taken it as a sign that she'd been able to…well, *hack* was sort of an ugly word, she preferred *access*…access his personnel files so easily. She knew he was divorced, she knew how much money he'd made, and once she had his Social Security number, with a little computer ingenuity, she even knew his net worth. But those weren't the really important things she'd discovered. Knowing both his zodiac sign and his year of birth, she'd run compatibility reports on her and Liam as a couple, both astrological and Chinese horoscope. It had been another green light when the reports said she and Liam were a well-matched pair. If that wasn't an important sign, she didn't know what was. She might be a military historian and know her way around a weapon or two and combat tactics, but she was a woman and a romantic at heart. The stars had ordained them as a couple.

She glanced around the room, which imparted a peacefulness. She ran her hand over the cotton squares, her fingers encountering the tiny ridges formed by rows of small, straight stitches connecting them. The squares were a soothing mix of florals and stripes in faded shades of lavender, yellow and rose. Ecru lace curtains hung at the window. A small yellow-and-rose braided rug was on the wood floor next to the bed. A lone framed watercolor hung on the wall. Snow-laden spruce branches bowed beneath their winter weight, while chickadees perched on the branches. A snow-shoe hare sat poised on the snowy ground. Rather than icy cold, the place embodied serenity. A small bowl of fresh lemon slices and dried lavender on the bedside nightstand perfumed the air.

She crossed to the window, pushing aside the lace curtain to look down at the small town nestled against a surreal backdrop of evergreens, distant mountains and blue sky. The sounds of life drifted up—childish laughter, a barking dog, the distinct hum of a diesel-engine truck, adult voices. A bird—she didn't know if it was a hawk, vulture or eagle, as bird identification wasn't her forte—seemed to float on a wind current in the distance.

Biting back a sigh at the utter tranquility around her, she made her way down the hall to the communal bathroom Merilee had pointed out. Ten minutes later, she was back downstairs in the airstrip office and had gotten the rundown on the restaurant/bar next door and the rest of the town's accommodations and attractions.

"I think I'd like to book a massage at that day spa." She might as well make the most of her time here.

"You can either drop by or I can call for you."

Mallory hesitated. "I'll just drop by.

"Sure. It's easy to find." Merilee Swenson laughed. "Everything here is easy to find."

There was much to be said for easy to find but that didn't always get you what you wanted. Liam Reinhardt had been easy enough to find. Yet another indication they belonged together. Once they met, she was sure he'd know it, too.

5

TANSY BRUSHED ON another coat of mascara and checked herself in the mirror, leaning in close to peer without the aid of her glasses. Good, no clumps. The screen door slammed next door.

She left the bathroom and went to the kitchen window. Liam was heading toward the lake, barefoot again. She checked her watch. Yep, same time he'd gone for a swim yesterday. Sheer cussedness kept her at the window. She'd always had a streak of cussedness but something about Alaska was really bringing it out in her. Perhaps it was because everything seemed a little more authentic, a little stripped of the veneer of polite society here.

Okay, and she had to be honest with herself. She wanted to see him naked again. Who was she kidding? She wanted to feel him naked against her, in her. And the dreadful man knew it. And she didn't know if she was appalled or gratified that he wanted her, as well.

He'd watched her last night, seen her touch herself. And the beast had known she was thinking of him, imagining his fingers plying her slick folds, wanting him on her, in her, taking her hard and fast.

The intensity, the raw sexual want she'd seen in his eyes today… Bradley had never looked at her like that. No man had ever looked at her like that. And it was heady, potent, thoroughly confusing stuff.

She watched him now, even though she should turn away and go about her business. Again, he methodically disrobed and stood tall and proud at the water's edge. Broad shoulders, trim waist, a perfect butt giving way to strong thighs and muscled calves.

Want warred with reason. Want won. Arousal, barely held at bay, gripped her. She'd been wet with desire ever since that encounter at the line today. Simply the heat of his breath against her ear, the scent of sweat and man, had nearly driven her mad as she stood toe-to-toe with him. She wanted to know the feel of his skin beneath her fingertips, against her belly and thighs. She longed for his taste, for the warmth of his breath against her skin, his mouth on her breasts, the press of him inside her.

He walked into the water and she turned away. She was losing her mind to so desperately crave the touch of a man she didn't even like. He was angry and hard and who needed that bundle of trouble? Certainly not her.

Tansy reconsidered. She wasn't losing her mind. It was simply that Bradley had screwed with her head. He'd undermined her sense of self. Her attraction to Sergeant Reinhardt was rebound, pure and simple.

Determined to get over herself…and Bradley…and the odious Liam…she marched back into her bedroom and changed into the prettiest dress she owned. She was short and needed to drop ten pounds but the flowing cut of the dress accentuated her waist and camouflaged her excess baggage below. She slipped her feet into matching flats and, deciding to go for broke, put in her contacts. She usually didn't bother, but tonight she was on a mission. Tonight, if she was in rebound mode, she'd find someone other than Liam to rebound with, on, or whatever the appropriate preposition might be.

Thursday nights were karaoke night at Gus's and she'd had a heck of a good time last week. Tonight, she, Jenna and Jenna's husband, Logan, were meeting there for an early dinner and then karaoke entertainment. Thursday night was Jenna and Logan's date night. Baby Emma had a sitter. So, she'd meet them and maybe, just maybe, she'd meet another rebound candidate that would get her off of this path of hell-bound insanity with Liam.

She brushed on a light coating of lip gloss and took stock of herself. Not bad. Good, in fact. She looked pretty. She felt pretty. She was ready to set forth and conquer. For good measure and extra fortification, she spritzed on some perfume.

She picked up her purse and walked out the door, locking it behind her. She paused as she opened the door to her borrowed vehicle.

Liam was still swimming laps, his arms slicing through the water, his shoulder and back muscles rippling like some athletic verse of poetry. Under different circumstances, she would've been neighborly and invited the idiot in the water to go with her, offered him a ride into town. But they weren't different circumstances, so she left him to his own devices in the lake and climbed into the FJ Cruiser.

She didn't glance back as she drove down the driveway.

She hoped he drowned in his own solitude. Well, metaphorically speaking, not literally.

Let the lout wonder just where she'd gone...and if she'd be back.

LIAM ENTERED GUS'S, once again in a brooding, dark state. Finally, Wellington had vacated the premises but he'd foolishly allowed Bull and Merilee to talk him into joining them for dinner tonight. He'd figured he at least owed them that much since they'd hooked him up with a place to stay and a job.

The joint was hopping. Games were going at a couple of pool tables in the back corner and a dartboard. Most of the tables and all of the booths were taken, as were most of the stools at the bar. On the jukebox, Elvis sang "Love Me Tender." He figured Gus's ranked two steps below a honky-tonk—it sure wouldn't qualify as fine dining.

The question as to where Wellington had taken her quirky, well-rounded ass was quickly answered. Despite the crowded room, he spotted her immediately across the way. The woman had a way of showing up front and center in his scope.

She sat at a table with Jenna and a dark-haired man Liam hadn't met. Maybe he was Wellington's date.

She was certainly all dolled up tonight, although Liam preferred her wearing her glasses. There was something kind of sexy about her specs—that schoolteacher/library male fantasy thing. The scent of her perfume had hung in the evening air when he'd walked back to the cabin from his swim.

Maybe she'd take the man beside her back to her cabin tonight. Better yet, maybe the man would take her to his place and Liam would have the whole parcel of land to himself, just the way he wanted. Yeah, that'd be grand. Perfect.

She was laughing at something the man said when she spotted Liam. She deliberately turned back to her date, as if she hadn't seen Liam at all. Good.

Rather belatedly he noticed Merilee and Bull sitting two tables over. Merilee waved him their way. Liam made his way through the tables to them. The two empty chairs faced Wellington...and her date. No biggie. He sat down. "Evening," he said.

Merilee reached over and placed her hand on his. "I'm so glad you're joining us this evening." She squeezed. "I'm glad you're here."

"So am I. Thanks for the invite tonight." There wasn't much else he could say under the circumstances.

Merilee shook her head. "I wasn't thinking. You and Tansy could've shared a ride. I should've known she was going to meet Jenna and Logan here tonight. Have you met Logan yet?"

Logan must be the date. Wellington had certainly pulled out all the stops for him. "Not yet."

"Well, there's no time like the present," Merilee said. Merilee was really into that introduction business. Liam actually had no interest in meeting Logan. She was in the process of pushing back from the table when Bull spoke up.

"It can wait, Merilee," Bull said. He nodded at Liam across the table. "Liam's going to be here awhile. He can't meet everyone at once. Let him settle in first."

"Okay." She pushed her chair back into place and said to her husband, "You're right." She rolled her eyes across the table at Liam. "Sometimes I hate it when he's right."

Bull nodded with a grin. "I'm always right."

Liam laughed. Bull and Merilee were good together. He and Natalie had never been that, never had between them what his aunt and uncle seemed to have. Hell, they'd been together for twenty-five years. And who exactly was this Logan? "Sure. I can meet him later. Who is he?"

"He's Jenna's husband," Merilee said. Ah. "He splits his time between here and Georgia but he's mostly here since their baby arrived in June."

If Logan wasn't Wellington's date, then who the hell was she all gussied up for?

"You'll have to meet baby Emma, too," Merilee said. She caught herself. "You do like babies, don't you?"

Well, he didn't actually know. He'd never spent much time around them. He and Natalie had talked about maybe starting a family one day, but that day had never come. He figured it was just as well considering how their marriage had turned out. He sure as hell wasn't at a point in his rudderless life right now where it was even on his radar.

"Uh, I guess I like babies well enough." He grinned at Merilee. "I don't dislike them, so does that count?"

He could feel Wellington watching him. He kept his attention trained on Merilee.

Merilee chuckled. "We'll give you points for not disliking them."

The waitress, a pretty redhead appropriately named Ruby, stopped by and took their drink orders. "You ready to order dinner or do you need a minute?"

"We might want to get it in now. They're pretty slammed," Merilee said.

"We've got lasagna, caribou stew and bison burgers with fries."

"Because Thursday nights are so popular, there are only three choices," Bull explained to Liam. "The caribou and bison are local."

Liam had noticed Wellington working on a burger at her table. And the woman soaked a fry in catsup. It was almost sexual the way she ate her fries. Damn distracting was what it was.

Liam, Bull and Merilee all opted for the burgers and Ruby hurried off.

"Everything go okay with Sven today?" Bull said.

"Oh, yeah. He's a good guy. He's got a top-notch crew, too."

His uncle nodded. "I thought it'd be a good fit."

"And you're happy with the cabin at Shadow Lake?" Merilee joined in.

"Couldn't ask for anything nicer."

"Isn't Tansy just a doll?"

Liam glanced over at the doll in question and then back to Merilee. That wasn't quite how he thought of Wellington, but the easiest, least red-flagging course of action was to agree. "Absolutely."

"So, you two are getting along okay?"

He glanced her way again. A smile, directed at Logan, lit her face. Liam looked away. "Like a house afire." There was definitely heat there, white-hot heat.

Merilee smiled. "When I heard about the sand, I wasn't too sure."

How'd she know? Shadow Lake was a couple of

miles out of town and set back from the main road. It was pretty much to itself.

Bull looked at him. "Son, I told you yesterday, news travels fast here."

Damn. No kidding it spread fast. "It was a joke." He shot another look over at Wellington, who was chatting up a storm. "She's got a heck of a sense of humor." It *had* been damn funny. She did have a sense of humor.

Merilee smiled. "That's a side of her I haven't really seen, but a sense of humor goes a long way in life."

Every now and then the husky notes of Wellington's voice would drift over, not that he could actually hear what she was saying, not that he wanted to.

"I hear Lars is coming," Bull said. "You mind if he stays with you or would you rather us put him up with us?"

Crap. He'd forgotten that his twin was taking leave and coming to see him. How the hell could he have driven all the way to Alaska and still not manage to get away from life and everyone? But since Lars was coming to see Liam, the onus fell on him. "He can stay with me."

Ruby arrived with the bison burgers and they all dug in. Between carrying Sheetrock and his swim, he'd worked up an appetite. Half an hour later they'd finished dinner, the meal having been spent on conversation about the town. Merilee had recounted how she and Bull had finally gotten hitched in a Christmas Day ceremony a year and a half ago.

She knew how to spin a yarn. Liam gave her kudos for not asking him the questions about him and Natalie that were lurking in the back of her eyes. Sooner or later she would, but he was glad it was later. He didn't want to talk about the past and how he'd wound up where he was now—no career, no wife and no home.

Throughout the meal, Wellington had remained in his line of sight, in the distance, beyond the gap between Merilee and Bull. A couple of different people had stopped by their table to chat, but no one had dropped into and stayed in the seat next to her. Maybe Wellington didn't have a hot assignation after all.

While Tansy had been on his central radar, the sixth sense that had served him so well in combat had been prickling from another area of the room. He turned. A woman, tall with straight blond hair that fell just past her shoulders, sat at the bar. He'd never laid eyes on her. She shot him a smile. He smiled back and then turned around. He wasn't interested.

In the far corner, near the pool tables, a long-haired Native fellow he'd met yesterday, Nelson Sisnukett, hopped up on the small stage tucked there. He picked up a microphone. "Welcome to karaoke night at Gus's."

Hell, no. He was just about to excuse himself when Merilee beamed in his direction. "This is fun. Everyone really gets into it."

He could hardly leave on that note.

Nelson continued talking. "We're going to start out with a real treat tonight. Jefferson Walker Monroe is gonna blow his horn for us."

The well-dressed man with the white hair who'd been on the other side of the chessboard took the stage, saxophone in hand, to a rousing round of applause.

Merilee addressed someone over Liam's shoulder as the smoky notes of the saxophone carried through the room. "Hi. Are you having a good time?"

"I am." It was the blonde from the bar. "There are lots of interesting people here."

"Why don't you join us, unless you're already with some of the folks at the bar?"

"I'd love to, if I'm not intruding."

"Not at all," Merilee said. "This is my husband, Bull Swenson, and our nephew Liam Reinhardt. Liam, Bull, this is Mallory Kincaid. She just arrived from New Orleans today."

She had the classic girl-next-door look. Shoulder-length hair, slightly square jaw, nice complexion. A smattering of freckles dusted her nose. Liam would put her in her mid- to late-twenties. Damn nice figure, too. Tall, athletic build.

She was strikingly pretty. And he didn't feel even a remote interest in her. Given all his sexual energy earlier, none of it transferred to the pretty woman next to him.

She nodded a greeting as she slipped into the empty seat. "Mr. Swenson, Mr. Reinhardt, it's nice to meet you."

"Liam just got into town yesterday," Merilee said.

"Oh, really?" She turned her gaze to him. Her eyes were shamrock-green. "Is it just a visit or are you here to stay?"

"Not sure yet. How about you?"

"Oh, I'm just here for a few days to enjoy the Alaskan wilderness."

He didn't know the woman but there was something studied about her casualness. She'd approached their table deliberately. He was pretty damn sure she'd manipulated the invitation.

Even though she was a stranger, he couldn't shake the sense she had an agenda and it involved him.

"Did you get by the spa for an appointment?" Merilee asked.

"I sure did. I'm down for the works tomorrow at two."

Across the way, Wellington was checking out the blonde, surreptitiously, but checking her out nonetheless.

Jefferson finished his sax solo and the first singing act took to the stage. An older woman started her version of an old Patsy Cline tune, "Crazy." It wasn't as bad as it could have been. She actually had a decent voice.

He stayed through the song and then pushed his chair back. He'd fulfilled his social obligations and then some. Tansy was still sitting with Jenna and Logan. However, she wasn't smiling now. Her expression was definitely tight. He supposed "Crazy" was a hard song to sit through when a breakup was still fresh. Regardless, he was getting out of here before the next act started.

"I'm heading out. Early morning. I enjoyed dinner." He nodded to Mallory. "Nice to meet you."

"Nice to meet you, as well. Maybe we'll bump into each other again."

"Maybe."

He stood and made his way toward the door.

He was halfway there when the door opened and his cousin Dirk strolled in. Damn, what was this, old home week? He hadn't seen his cousin since Liam and Natalie had tied the knot. He knew Dirk had been in town, but then he'd left for parts unknown. Dirk looked rough. Liam almost didn't recognize him. His hair was down to his shoulders and an unkempt beard covered his face. But beneath all the hair, the square of his jaw and his eyes remained unmistakable.

A smile that didn't bode well curled Dirk's lips. "I heard you were here."

Jesus, he might as well have taken out a full-page ad.

"I heard you'd been here."

"Yeah? Well, I'm back. I've got something for you. This is for Natalie."

The last thing Liam knew was an exploding pain as Dirk's fist connected with Liam's face.

6

TANSY JUMPED TO HER FEET, along with pretty much everyone else in the room. The music stopped. All eyes were trained on the doorway and the drama unfolding there.

One minute Liam had been standing, the next he was laid out on the floor. The big hairy man who'd punched him simply stood there rubbing his fist with his other hand.

Bull made his way through the gawkers and walked over. "You feel better now, Dirk?" he asked. "I hope so because that's enough. You're done."

On the floor, Liam showed signs of life. He sat up, shaking his head to clear it, his hand to his jaw. Blood trickled down his face. He'd caught his cheek on a chair edge on the way down.

Dirk looked from Liam to Bull. "Yep, I'm done. I said what I needed to say."

Merilee had gone to stand beside Bull. "Say?" She raised an eyebrow.

Dirk grinned unrepentantly. "You know actions speak louder than words."

"You gonna take that, Reinhardt?" a male voice from somewhere behind Tansy called out.

A chorus of male murmurs followed.

"Quit crowing, Rooster," Merilee said to the man in the back. "And the rest of you hush up, too."

Dirk stepped closer to Liam and held out his hand, offering him help up. Liam looked from Dirk's hand up to his face. "We're even."

Even though it wasn't a question, Dirk nodded his agreement. "We're even."

Liam took the proffered hand and rose to his feet. Blood running down his face, he grinned. "You just used your free pass." He rubbed his hand over his jaw. "You've obviously been working out."

"Been up on the pipeline."

"I hate to break up the family reunion here," Merilee offered drily, "but you're dripping blood on Lucky's floor and this is an eating establishment." She handed him a paper napkin to staunch the blood.

"Sorry," Liam said, holding it to the cut on his face.

Nelson approached, having turned his karaoke emceeing duties over to a short balding man. "Dr. Skye's out delivering a baby who decided to show up early but let's step next door and get you cleaned up. You might need a stitch or two."

Dirk, Bull, Merilee, Liam and Nelson all exited through the door that connected the airstrip to the restaurant/bar. And the pretty blonde woman—Merilee had said her name was Mallory Kincaid and she had just arrived in town today—after a second or two, followed them into the airstrip.

Tansy's stomach felt as if it was tied up in a knot.

She sat back down, as did everyone else, and the conversation resumed, ramped up a notch with the drama.

"That was interesting," Jenna said.

"It was definitely unexpected. Who was that? What was it about?"

"I know they're cousins, but I have no clue what that was about."

Logan laughed. "No worries, honey. You will. Before midday tomorrow," he said.

Jenna flashed him an impish grin. "I know." She looked at Tansy. "I saw that look on your face. Mallory's staying at the bed-and-breakfast. That's why she went in behind them."

Right. Tansy said, "Did you see the way she was looking at Liam?"

"I sure did. She was watching him from the bar like a hungry cat eyeing a canary."

Logan looked from Jenna to Tansy and back to Jenna. "I think I missed something."

Jenna rubbed his shoulders. "Of course you did, sweetie. You're a man. But if there's one thing women don't miss, it's when another woman is interested in a man. And Mallory Kincaid is interested in Liam."

He shook his head. "If you say so."

Jenna laughed. "I know so."

Tansy felt kind of queasy inside. She must've eaten too much of Lucky's delicious bison burger and fries. Mallory Kincaid was everything Tansy wasn't—tall, thin, blonde—and Liam hadn't pulled his hostile act with her. "Yeah, she was definitely putting out signals."

"It won't do her any good."

"Why?" Obviously Jenna knew something Tansy didn't.

"Because he's not interested in her."

"He didn't seem not interested in her," Tansy said.

Jenna cocked her head to one side and looked at Tansy as if she'd just climbed off of a spaceship. "How could he be interested in her when he was busy watching you all night?"

"No, he wasn't." He'd looked at her when he'd walked in and then ignored her all night.

"Tansy Patrice Wellington, the man couldn't stop looking at you all evening. Of course, you didn't see because you were so busy trying to ignore him." Jenna looked at Logan. "Am I right?"

Logan held up his hands in mock surrender. "I have no clue. You know I'm not good at that stuff. In fact, I'm going to go over and check with Leo on a new stock offering."

"You do that, honey, but don't talk business too long. We'll wrap up our girl business soon."

Jenna's husband was all about finance and had found a kindred spirit in retired insurance salesman turned general store owner Leo Perkins. Logan simply shook his head as if he didn't quite know what to make of his wife and headed to the other table. Jenna scootched her chair closer to Tansy's.

"Now, while Logan's gone, tell me what's going on with Liam."

"I told you last night when I called about the sand, he's got some issue with me being out at Shadow Lake. He thinks I'm going to compromise his privacy. He's a jerk."

"Really? I think he's the best thing that could've possibly happened."

Jenna was a smart lady, but she seemed off the mark

this time. "I'm obviously missing a piece of some puzzle here. How's that?"

"You got a lot of work done today, even with the sand being delivered, didn't you? You haven't been thinking about Bradley nearly as much, have you?"

That was all true. "How'd you know?"

"You haven't mentioned either work or Bradley tonight. If you're not mentioning work, it means it's good. If you haven't mentioned Bradley, it means you're not thinking about him. And I think you're not thinking about him because you're distracted by Liam." Jenna beamed. "I think he's just what you need to get you over Bradley and finish your book."

A delicious shiver ran through her at the remembered heat in Liam's eyes and the fire he stoked in her. Trepidation followed fast on the heels of anticipation. "You mean, like a rebound?"

"Sure. It's the way things work. You throw a basketball against something and what happens? It bounces back. It rebounds. Sooner or later you've got to rebound. Liam could fit that bill."

"I don't know if I want to rebound yet or if I'm ready."

"Don't sweat it. You'll know when the time is right." Jenna smiled and waggled her eyebrows à la Groucho Marx. "But there is that saying that there's no time like the present."

Before Tansy could comment, and quite frankly she didn't know what to say to that, Merilee slipped into the chair next to Tansy. "Nelson says Liam doesn't need stitches, just a butterfly bandage, but he really whacked the back of his head. He doesn't think Liam should drive. That, of course, has made Liam act like a bear with a sore paw. Can you haul him home since he's right next door?"

Oh, joy. He'd definitely be difficult now, but she could hardly say no. "Sure. No problem."

"Well, not to cut your evening short, but Nelson's almost done with him. I think if he's left to cool his jets too long, he'll just get on his motorcycle and go."

Tansy gathered her purse. "I was just about to leave anyway. I need to let Jenna and Logan get on with their date night."

Jenna laughed, looking around the crowded room. "Oh, yeah, 'cause you were keeping us from being alone. Go take the wounded soldier home. Why put off to tomorrow what you can do today?"

Merilee looked a little confused but pretty much everyone was used to not fully following Jenna conversationally at some point or another.

Tansy, however, knew exactly what her stepsister meant.

THE LIGHTS OF GOOD Riddance faded in the side view mirror as Wellington headed out to Shadow Lake. Neither of them had said a word since she'd met him at the door outside of the airstrip/bed-and-breakfast.

Her perfume, her very presence, seemed to wrap around him in the confines of the SUV and the night.

"Go ahead and say it, Wellington," Liam said, his injured cheek throbbing.

Her profile was etched darker than the dark of the night. "What is it I'm supposed to say, Reinhardt?"

"Don't you want to know why he hit me? Don't you want to crow that I've dogged you about you being next door and now you're taking me home?"

"I don't do smug." Her voice sounded huskier than usual in the dark.

"Right." She'd been so smug about her line in the sand she could hardly stand herself.

"As to why your cousin knocked you out—" she *would* have to phrase it that way "—that's between you and him. I don't want to interject myself in your business. I know how you feel about your privacy."

"I'm beginning to think there's no such thing here." The gossip would be all over Good Riddance before sunrise.

"It didn't help that he did it in front of everyone in Gus's on a crowded night. Since there'll be all kinds of speculation and your privacy's already shot to heck, I'll bite. Why'd he hit you?"

"He thinks I stole his girl."

"Did you?"

"Not knowingly. I didn't know at the time he was interested in Natalie. Dirk's not the best communicator."

"It must run in the family," she said with a note of teasing. Touché. She followed it with a laugh. "He expressed himself pretty clearly tonight." She glanced at him and then looked back to the road. "What happened to Natalie?"

"We got a divorce."

"Oh, wow. You didn't just steal his girl for a date, you *married* her and then it still didn't work out."

Wellington didn't sugarcoat it, but that was fine, he didn't need sugarcoating. But he would set the record straight on one point. "I didn't steal her. I don't poach on other men's territory."

"No, you don't seem like the type of man who would," she said quietly. Her hands were small and dainty against the steering wheel. Her bare arms were graceful.

"By the way, you look nice tonight."

Was that faint sound an indrawn breath?

"Thank you. He must've hit you harder than I thought. You actually said something nice to me."

"But I like you better with your glasses on."

"That's more like it, Reinhardt."

It was the truth so why'd she sound as if her nose was suddenly out of joint? "So, did you have a date tonight who didn't show?"

"No. I did not get stood up, thank you very much. I did not have a date."

"Why else would you get all dolled up?"

"Maybe because I wanted to and I can. I don't have to 'doll up,' as you call it, for anyone but me."

Natalie had had some book about men being from one planet and women from another. He'd thought it was a bunch of crap at the time she'd run around quoting from it, but honestly women just didn't make sense sometimes. "So, you didn't have a date tonight?"

She turned onto the private road leading to the cabins.

"I'm going to cut you some slack because you suffered a concussion." Actually, Wellington was proving to be good entertainment. "No, I did not have a date tonight. And what business is it of yours?"

She threw the vehicle in Park and killed the engine.

"None. Just passing time." He opened the door and got out while she did the same. She rounded the back end of the SUV and he headed to his cabin as she mounted the stairs. He paused to make sure she got in without mishap. She opened the door.

"Thanks for the ride," he said, his foot on the bottom stair of his cabin. "Oh, and feel free to undress in front of the window again tonight. I enjoy the view."

"Wait up for it," she responded with a sweetness he didn't trust. The door closed behind her.

Half an hour later he lay in bed, in the dark, his blind up and window cracked, doing just that. He waited to see what Wellington would do, because she would do something.

Five minutes later she snapped on the bedside lamp, her blinds drawn, throwing her into relief the same as last night. However, unlike last night, this time she climbed on the bed on her knees. He swallowed hard. Damn.

The intercom next to his bed rang, the one that looked like an old-fashioned phone and ran between the two cabins, and he picked it up. "Yes?"

"Are you watching? Are you up?"

He was both. "Yes."

"I just wanted to make sure." The intercom clicked in his ear. She'd hung up.

He watched, waiting, unblinking.

Slowly, languidly, her movements heavy with deliberateness, she raised her right arm and his breath stuck in his chest.

Her movements still seductive, she presented her hand...and then her middle finger.

He blinked and burst out laughing as she extinguished her light. Damn. Laughing hurt his head.

Wellington had flipped him off.

It had been better than another striptease.

He settled against his pillow. Well, *almost* better than a striptease.

THE FOLLOWING AFTERNOON Tansy dropped by the airstrip office to say hello to Merilee after her lunch at Gus's. Alberta was parked in the chair next to Merilee's desk, while Dwight and Jefferson, Lord Byron on the floor between them, contemplated life and the chessboard.

"How's it shaking, sugar?" Alberta quipped as Tansy crossed the room.

Tansy laughed, feeling more carefree than she had in some time. "It's shaking just fine. And you?"

"The sun rose this morning and me and Dwight lived to see it. Can't ask for much more than that at our age, except for a good roll in the sack now and then." She winked. "How's that man of yours after his beat down last night?"

Tansy felt the heat of a blush creeping up her face. "He's not my man," she said, "but he was fine on the way back last night. I heard Sven stop by this morning and pick him up for work."

He'd been out for his run before that. Apparently a knockout didn't stop Liam Reinhardt, even if it had kept him from driving the previous evening.

Merilee shook her head. "Men. Liam and Dirk were just fine afterwards."

Tansy laughed. "It gave the town something to talk about. Gus's was buzzing just now." Jenna hadn't been available for lunch but Tansy had just listened to all the chatter around her. No one was malicious, but the place had been rife with speculation. Tansy had simply kept her mouth shut. Reinhardt's news wasn't hers to tell.

Her days were beginning to take on a nice rhythm. This morning she'd actually made more headway rather than floundering on her work. Coming in for lunch at Gus's had been a nice break rather than the escape from writer's block that it had previously been. She'd found some measure of hope that she might actually make her deadline with some decent material to boot. And on a larger level, she had the sense that she was reorienting herself in her life.

Alberta was about to say something when Mallory Kincaid came down the stairs from the bed-and-breakfast upstairs. Merilee introduced them.

Tansy shook the other woman's hand, her stomach knotting. That little measure of Zen she'd come in with dissipated in the other woman's presence.

"It's nice to meet you," the blonde said.

"Nice to meet you, as well." Tansy did not find it nice to meet the other woman, but she'd been reared too well not to be polite. Something about Mallory bugged her. There was just something that didn't quite sit right with her.

Mallory was even worse in person. She possessed a lilting musical voice, arresting green eyes and at least five inches, maybe six, on Tansy's meager five-foot-four stature.

"So, are you off to Jenna's for your spa date?" Merilee said.

"I am." Mallory smoothed her hand over the edge of her shirt. She looked casual but put-together. "I'm really looking forward to it."

"I'm sure you'll love it," Merilee said. She added, "Tansy and Jenna are sisters."

"Oh." Mallory's green eyes widened in surprise. "I would've never guessed."

The other woman wasn't being bitchy, but somehow her genuine surprise stung more than if it had contained an element of cattiness. "We're technically stepsisters, which is why there's no resemblance."

"Ah." Mallory nodded. "I have a stepsister, as well, and her mom is Asian so Dina and I seriously don't resemble each other. Do you live here?"

"Just visiting for a bit."

"She's staying in one of the cabins out at Shadow Lake along with Liam," Alberta said with a mischievous gleam in her eye.

"Oh. I didn't realize…"

That caught Mallory even more off guard than the Jenna situation. Tansy cleared up the misunderstanding. "She means he's in the cabin next to mine."

"Oh, I see." Tansy so did not imagine the flicker of relief in Mallory's eyes and the faint shadow of hostility. "Shadow Lake sounds interesting. Perhaps I could stop by one afternoon to check it out."

Ha. More like check Liam out…and Tansy considered it pretty darn pushy. Not that Liam was any of Tansy's business, but she wasn't about to have her work interrupted, especially when she was finally cranking on it again, just so some strange woman could put herself in the man's path. No, thanks. "Sorry, I work long hours. If I'm not here in town, then I'm working."

"Well, perhaps we can work something out on a day you won't be too busy. Maybe tomorrow."

Good grief. Was she going to have to tattoo *no* on her forehead? The woman was relentless. "Sorry, but I really need to stick with it. I'm avoiding distractions." And pushy strangers she didn't care for. Settled. Done. She didn't like this woman.

"Well, better run. I don't want to be late for my pampering."

"Enjoy," Merilee said as Mallory was walking out.

Juliette came through the door, her pup, Baby, by her side, passing Mallory on her way out.

"She's definitely not shy," Alberta said with a snort as the door closed behind Mallory.

Juliette looked bewildered. "Did I miss something?"

"Just a little woman-to-woman standoff," Alberta said with a smirk.

"It was nothing," Tansy said. She had yet to see Juliette without the pup. She and Sven were funny. Baby was with her today and Sven's dog, Bruiser, went to work with him every day. Tansy had run into the couple and their canines twice last week when she'd gone for a late evening hike along the lake. Juliette and Tansy had sort of clicked and Tansy enjoyed chatting with the couple while the dogs cavorted. It was cute, but then again, Sven and Juliette made a cute couple. They obviously adored each other. Come to think of it, there was a lot of that going around in Good Riddance.

She bit back a sigh. It had been rather painful a week ago but now it was just nice. She supposed she was getting used to being split with Bradley and rethinking her life without him.

"Oh, okay," Juliette said, her gaze encompassing the room. She looked at Tansy with a quiet smile. "I just popped by Gus's looking for you, since I missed you at the cabin. I know it's last minute but Sven and I decided to cook out tonight and we thought you might want to come over for dinner." The last time she'd ran into them Sven had mentioned she ought to come over for a cookout before she left. "Would you care to join us?"

She'd be more than happy to get to know them better. "That sounds nice. What can I bring?"

Juliette shook her head. "Don't worry about bringing anything. I know you're not particularly in cook mode while you're here. And we're just doing simple."

"I can make brownies. I picked up a mix at the dry goods store when I first got here just in case a chocolate craving struck in the middle of the night." Or she needed to drown her sorrows in chocolate. However, Jenna had kept her stocked in cookies thus far.

Juliette laughed. "Okay. Sure. Bring brownies. Around seven? That gives Sven time to clean up after work."

Tansy was dying to know if they'd also invited her next-door neighbor but she could hardly ask. Part of her hoped he was there, part of her hoped he wasn't. And what she hoped didn't matter—if he was, he was. If he wasn't, well, then, he wasn't. Either way, she was going.

"Seven sounds perfect. I'll be there."

7

LIAM WALKED OUT his front door, a bottle of sparkling water that the dry goods store stocked specifically for Juliette tucked beneath his arm. Merilee had given him the heads-up on that one.

Wellington was just walking down her front steps, looking as pretty as she had the previous evening. She had on a purple dress that hit her right above her knees—Wellington had some nice, shapely legs. The dress flared out from the waist and sort of flowed over her hips. The color looked nice with her dark hair and olive-tinted skin.

Sven had said she was coming when he extended Liam's invite. Although socializing had been the last thing on Liam's want-to-do list, he felt somewhat obligated as Sven had given him a job. He'd show up tonight, as he'd shown up last night for dinner with Merilee and Bull, and then his obligations should all be satisfied and he could retreat back into solitude. Plus, he'd be damned if he'd have Wellington think his not showing up was retreat or defeat on his part. He was almost looking forward to the evening.

"I think you're going my way," he said. "Want a lift?"

She cut her eyes from him to the motorcycle and back to him. "On your motorcycle?"

"No, on my back. Of course on my motorcycle. It's how I get from point A to point B."

"You're so gracious, Reinhardt. Really. But I suppose it's asinine to take two vehicles."

"Hey, it's a nice evening. Just think of mine as a convertible without all the sides."

She laughed and the sound flowed over him, through him. "That's a different take, but okay. You certainly have a unique perspective on things."

"You might want to grab a jacket for the ride back."

"Okay. Hold the brownies. Wait. I can't hold on to the brownies and you at the same time."

"Got you covered. Go get your jacket." She looked ready to balk and he added, "Please. I'm starving, Wellington. I'm not nearly as fun-loving and carefree when I'm hungry."

"Well, we definitely want you at your best" was her smart-ass response as she handed off the brownies and turned to go back inside.

He put the brownies, along with the bottle of seltzer, in a backpack and strapped it to the bike.

Tansy returned within two minutes. The woman was efficient, he'd give her that.

She eyed his bike and then him. "So what do I do?"

"You've never been on a bike before?"

"Not a motorcycle."

"You'll like it."

"How would you know?"

"You will." He climbed on and looked over his shoulder. "Now you climb on the back and just hold on."

"I'm wearing a dress."

"Wellington, just shut up and climb on. Mind the pipes. They get hot fast."

She climbed on and cautiously settled her hands at his waist. However, there was very little room on the seat and he felt the press of her thighs against his hips and her breasts against his back.

"Don't we need helmets?"

"We're going about a mile and a half. It's fine. Just relax. Tuck the hem of your dress down or it's going to be up around your waist. Of course, with your exhibitionist tendencies, you might like that."

"Poor you. Considering how you like to watch, you'd miss the show. Speaking of, how'd you enjoy last night?" She dropped her voice to a lower seductive pitch on the last part. Pipes weren't the only thing on the bike getting hot fast.

"It was almost as good as the night before. I can't wait for tonight."

"Last night was the final curtain call."

"But your audience demands an encore. And you should always play to your audience and make sure they're satisfied."

"My audience is on their own."

"I never pegged you for a quitter."

"Funny. I never pegged you as a watcher. I'd have thought you were more a man of action."

"The key, Wellington, is in waiting until the right time to take action."

And that just about summed up life.

TANSY SIPPED THE lime-flavored seltzer and sank back into the Adirondack chair overlooking the lake. Sven and Liam were over tossing horseshoes in the horse-shoe pit. An array of wind chimes in assorted sizes, made of various materials, played in the breeze drifting off of the lake. The puppies, Bruiser and Baby, had exhausted themselves and were piled in a heap next to Juliette's chair.

"Dinner was delicious and this is just wonderful—very relaxing, very tranquil. I love your wind chime collection."

Juliette looked pleased. "Thanks. I make them."

"Seriously? They're lovely."

"It's just a hobby."

"Wow. Would you ever consider making them for other people? If I paid you, would you make one for me? My mom would love something like these."

"I never thought about making them for anyone else, except I did make one for Sven as a wedding gift."

"Nice. It's okay if it's not something you're comfortable with. I just think yours are really nice."

"Thanks. I'm glad you came for dinner. Sven and I are pretty quiet and sort of keep to ourselves but the weather's been so nice and he got a new grill so he's just been chomping at the bit."

Tansy laughed. "He was really into grilling." Sven and Liam had approached grilling as if it were some delicate maneuver to be executed under stringent conditions.

Juliette smiled, her feelings for her husband all over her face. "They're just such men, aren't they?"

"You got that right. There's lots of testosterone floating around over there."

Juliette sighed. "It's great, isn't it?"

"Uh, yeah, I guess."

"Once you get used to all that testosterone, you'll never go back to the metrosexual side."

Tansy paused for a moment and then she just burst out laughing. Juliette simply smiled. "I...that was just..." Tansy said once her laughter died. "I so didn't expect you to say that."

Bradley was so very metrosexual, which had been one of the things she'd loved about him—his quiet, gentle spirit, the fact that she could use his hair gel and didn't have to bring over her own. And there was a part of her that felt a bit of a panic that he was slipping away from her. She really hadn't thought about him all evening. She'd been totally tuned in to the here and now. She'd found that Liam actually did have a charming side. She'd nearly fallen over when he'd pulled out and held her chair at dinner, when he'd paused and allowed her to precede him through a door. He had charm and he had manners, when he cared to pull them out and dust them off. His leg had brushed against hers beneath the table at dinner. Now and again his arm had glanced against hers, or he'd leaned in at the same time she had and his breath had been warm against her skin. And always there was the memory of his hips against her thighs, the expanse of his back against her breasts, his scent in her nose, the press of his shoulder against her face, blocking too much wind from her. There was the memory of the ride over...and the promise of the return trip to the cabins.

And much as she didn't want to admit it, there had been a "couple" feel to the evening. It had been like some aberration of a blind date, except they did sort of know each other.

The evening drew to a close. Juliette had the weekend flight schedule, so Tansy and Liam made their way back to his motorcycle.

"We'll have to do it again sometime soon."

"That would be fun. I really had a good time."

Liam climbed on the bike and she climbed on behind him. She liked the wind in her hair, the throb of the motor, and heaven help her but she also liked the press of him against her.

They pulled into the yard, the headlight picking out the bright eyes and rounded shape of a porcupine. The animal took off in the other direction. Liam killed the engine.

They both climbed off of the bike. Tansy thought she should just say thanks and walk away. What was she, a glutton for punishment, that she didn't just walk over to her own cabin, where the light on the porch spilled over the edge of the rail? Instead, she was reluctant for the night to end. There was something almost anticlimatic about quietly retreating to her cabin at the end of the evening.

"Thanks for the ride."

"You liked it?"

"I did."

"I knew you would. Maybe one afternoon we could go for a long ride."

Why was he asking her? "I think I would like that."

"Wellington…"

"Reinhardt…"

"I think we called a cease-fire this evening."

"I never declared war in the first place."

"But you drew the line in the sand. And look, now you've crossed the line, Wellington, which leaves me only one thing to do."

Her heart pounded in her chest. "What's that?"

"This..." Liam threaded his fingers through her hair, fitting his palm to the contours of her scalp. She tingled all over with anticipation—oh, yes, she knew what was coming, what she'd wanted for what felt like an eternity but in actuality had only been a couple of days.

His touch was surprisingly gentle. Tansy placed her palm against his chest and slid it up to his shoulder. She would not retreat. She wanted this thing too badly. However, she would not simply submit. She would meet him, participate.

His lips settled against hers, firm, warm. She sighed into the kiss and returned it, her lips seeking, exploring.

And then the kiss detonated. Like some time-released action, it exploded into heat and passion and fire, which raced through her, threatening to consume her. He pulled her hard against him and she pressed closer still.

Liam pulled away, his breathing ragged. "Good night, Wellington."

And then as quickly as it had started, it was over and she was still standing rooted to the spot when he quietly closed his cabin door behind him.

LIAM PACED ACROSS THE floor of the cabin, his boots resounding on the wood in the night's quiet. He was tight and hard and wanted Tansy Wellington. And the fervor with which she had returned his kiss made it fairly apparent that she wanted him, as well. And for this point in time, wanting her outweighed his need for privacy. She was leaving in a couple of weeks, so why not just go for it? It would be an uncomplicated win-win scenario.

He made up his mind and crossed to the door. Yanking it open, he found her standing on the other side, her hand raised to knock. Without a word, he pulled her inside and closed the door.

She leaned back against the door. "I want more," she said.

"How much more?"

"Just what you're willing to give for now." She drew a deep breath. "I need a distraction. You make me forget…other things."

Her former fiancé? He could live with that. Being a distraction was perfect. She wasn't asking for something he couldn't deliver.

He nodded, bracing one hand against the wood behind her, and plied his thumb against the soft round of her cheek. "I understand wanting a distraction. I could use the same thing."

He leaned in, summoned by her scent and the woman herself. Liam nuzzled the soft skin below her ear, enjoying the play of her hair against his face. He felt her tremble. He wasn't sure if it was excitement or fear, or perhaps a bit of both. It didn't matter. He wouldn't hurt her and inherently she knew that or she wouldn't have come seeking him, the same as he had been on his way to find her.

He kissed her. Her lips welcomed him, greeted him, opened to him. She wound her arms around his neck, finding the edge of his hair with her fingertips. She tasted like brownies and sweet, sweet woman.

Liam deepened the kiss and she opened her mouth to him, her tongue meeting his. He pressed against her, wanting to lose himself in her softness, the fullness of her breasts, the curves of her hips, the plumpness of her thighs.

She murmured indistinctly into his mouth and leaned into him fully.

Liam wrapped his arms around her and, mouths still fused, worked their way to the sofa. She touched him as if she couldn't get enough of him. She ran her hands beneath his shirt, her fingers as eager and seeking as her tongue in his mouth.

He explored the curves of her hips with his hands. He dragged his mouth down the column of her throat to the ridge of her collarbone. She felt, tasted, smelled so good. It had been so long. And she was as frantic as he was. He wasn't going to last long at this pace... but he wasn't sure he could slow down. But he'd damn well try. He pulled away from her, panting, as if he'd just run a half marathon in full battle gear.

"Tansy...I... Give me a second.... It's been a while...."

"Same here. I'm ready. Bring out the big gun, Reinhardt."

"What I'm trying to tell you is it's locked and loaded."

"Good. That's what I want. Now."

"Bedroom?"

"Too far."

He didn't need a second invitation. He freed himself from his jeans and underwear while she pulled down her panties. Her eyes glittered with heat and arousal.

"Oh, my. It *is* a big gun."

He leaned back and looked at her, the same as she was looking at him. She had a full bush and her pink sex glistened.

He'd always taken his time. He'd never simply had a woman after just a kiss or two—but then again, he didn't think he'd ever wanted a woman quite the way he wanted Tansy Wellington.

He positioned himself between her legs…and froze.

"Liam? What?"

"Condom. I don't have one."

"My purse. On the floor."

She reached down beside the couch and in less than a minute presented him with the cellophane-wrapped prophylactic. "You were saying…."

"Are you still—"

"Ready? Yes."

She looked wanton with her prim glasses and her legs splayed, her dress up around her thighs, eager for him. Damn this woman turned him on.

"You are one sexy woman."

She simply smiled and pulled him into position between her thighs. And then he was inside her. She was wet and tight and it was as if all the good things in life were right there between her thighs, wrapping around him, encompassing him.

"You feel good," he said.

"So do you. So. Do. You."

Liam stroked in and out. Hard and fast, which seemed to be what she wanted. She rose up to meet each of his thrusts with her own.

He gritted his teeth. He tried to hold out but it was futile. She felt too damn good.

He did something he'd never ever done before. He came too fast.

8

TANSY LAY BENEATH Liam, on the brink, but not there yet when he obviously had found his release. He had warned her ahead of time that he was in full firing position. It was, nonetheless, disappointing. Well, *frustrating* was a more apt word.

He rolled off her. "Hold that thought. I'll be right back."

He disappeared into the bathroom. She suddenly felt cold and exposed, the tweed fabric of the sofa rough beneath her bare skin. Disgruntled, she'd pulled her panties on, tugged her dress down over her thighs and sat back down on the couch. She'd wait until Liam returned before she left. That had been the most disappointing end to a most promising beginning. Forget sitting on the couch. She slipped her purse strap over her shoulder and stood, her legs not quite as steady as she would've liked.

He emerged from the bathroom, paused and then crossed the room to her.

"You don't follow orders very well," he said, but there was no sting in his comment. He reached out, slid her purse strap off of her shoulder and tossed it to the floor. "That is definitely not holding the thought."

He reached for her and she sidestepped him. "You're not obligated."

"No, I'm not *obligated*. I *want* to satisfy you, the way you satisfied me. I just got my round off too fast and needed to clean up." He took her by the hand and tried to lead her but she held her ground.

"I'll just head home."

"Tansy, we can do this my way or we can do this my way, but you are not walking out that door yet. Now, quit sulking and come here."

"I'm not sulking."

"Yes, you are. Damn, woman, it was embarrassing enough that I didn't have more willpower not to come so soon." She hadn't thought about it being embarrassing for him. And she hated that. It was one thing to both be in the throes of passion together, but now that he wasn't so hot and bothered, it just felt awkward. "But I'm not through with you yet."

It was possibly the least romantic, most straightforward verbal exchange she'd ever had regarding sex. Bradley had always been all about flowery phrases and candlelight. Oddly enough, Liam's *I'm not through with you yet* kind of turned her on.

"You're not through with me yet?"

"That's right. Actually, we're just getting started. Let's go to the bedroom."

Just getting started sounded promising, while walking out the door seemed a whole lot like cutting off her nose to spite her face. Tansy stepped forward and said, "Okay."

Liam's cabin was a mirror image of her own. Her

heart thumping against her chest, she followed him into the bedroom. The room furnishings were very similar to those next door. A double-bed was covered in a hand-made quilt, the headboard obviously hand-carved. A matching wardrobe was positioned against one wall in lieu of a closet. A single nightstand and a braided rug completed the furnishings. Unlike her bedroom next door, however, he didn't have any personal items scattered around. It was neat as a pin. The waning light filtered through lace curtains at the window, bathing the room in a mix of shadows and soft light.

He stopped by the bed. "Now, you were holding a thought," he said as he bent his head and kissed her neck. His mouth was warm, his lips firm against her sensitive skin. His whiskers rasped deliciously against her. The same sense of urgency, of want, she'd had before swept through her once again. She thrilled to the smell of him, the taste of him, the feel of him and the sound of his voice.

He pulled back the covers and they sank to the mattress's edge. He gentled her back onto the bed. While he kissed her, he ran his hand over her hip and beneath the hem of her dress. His touch, although sure and firm, wasn't in the least rough. Tansy sighed, relishing the stroke of his fingers against her flesh.

She arched up against his hands. Liam caught the edge of her panties with his finger and pulled them down her hips and the length of her legs. The air rushed cool against the heated flesh between her thighs.

He kissed the edge of her neck, the scrape of his whiskers sending shivers through her. He brushed his hand over her thigh as his mouth found her lips. Tansy wrapped her hand around his neck and pulled him closer, wielding her tongue against his. The intensity with which she wanted him increased, which she really hadn't thought was possible.

Liam stroked and touched her thighs, her lower belly, her hips. With one finger, he traced along the edge of her pubic mound. The maddening man touched everywhere but the one place she wanted him to touch the most. She pulled away from his mouth, panting. "Liam, you've got to—"

He shook his head and continued to circle her with his finger. "Patience."

Pouting, she fired back, "We've seen how much patience you had."

The infuriating man laughed at her. "Extenuating circumstances. Now, close your eyes."

"Maybe I don't want to."

"Just do it. For once, can you just do as instructed and not argue the point?"

Fine. If that's what it took for him to give her what she wanted…. She closed her eyes. He teased his tongue against the ridge of her collarbone, and the sensation arced through her, heaping fuel on the flame that was already burning inside her. Her eyes fluttered.

"Keep them closed," he said.

It really was more intense that way.

He captured her nipple in his mouth, clothes and all, and she sucked in her breath as the sensation shot straight through her to the aching need between her thighs. She dug her fingers in the muscles of his shoulders and moaned. He teased at her nipple with his teeth and she gasped. Tansy was nearly writhing with want when he finally touched his fingertip to her slick folds.

"Yes."

"Hmm." His sound of satisfaction reverberated through his mouth as he suckled her. He plucked and stroked at her flesh and she spread her legs farther apart, opening herself to his ministrations, her orgasm building. He slid a finger inside her and then another while he found her clitoris with his thumb.

She bit her lip when he curved his fingers inside her and rubbed a sensitive spot she hadn't even known existed. At the same time, he worked his thumb against her clitoris.

"I...oh...yes...please." Her cry of satisfaction reverberated around the room as waves of pleasure echoed through her body.

THE FOLLOWING DAY, MALLORY sighed in frustration as she rolled to her back and settled under the sheet, naked. Soothing flute music drifted on the air and candles lit the room. Jenna's spa was on par with any facility she'd find in the big city and certainly not what you'd anticipate in some backwoods town that didn't even have a traffic light. And she'd been comped her massage when she'd been bumped to today due to an overbooking. It was fine by her.

Ellie Sisnukett, newlywed and talented massage therapist, poured more warm oil into her hands. Ellie had a gifted touch. She'd told Mallory that she used to be a schoolteacher before she began working massage in Jenna's spa. If Ellie was half as good at teaching school as she was at massage, the little kiddies were missing out.

"You are so tense. Do you want to talk about it? Is it a man?"

"Isn't it always about a man?" She was getting a big

fat nowhere with initiating contact with Liam Reinhardt. Well, she'd met him but he was clearly not interested in small talk or chatting. It had been terribly disappointing that he hadn't immediately picked up on the rightness of her and him. Mallory, however, was convinced enough for both of them. So, it was simply time for her to lay her cards on the table. She'd tried subtle but subtle wasn't getting her anywhere. Liam was both personal and professional for her. "How did you meet your husband?"

"Nelson likes to say it was when he found me naked in Mirror Lake." Ellie laughed. "It's a thermal lake and I was there one night in the water naked when he showed up, but we'd known each other long before that. I actually dated his cousin Clint for a while. I'd always had a crush on Nelson but he'd never seemed to really notice me. But he noticed me then. We talked and really got to know each other and it just went from there."

"But what if a man is interested in someone else?"

Mallory had banked on Liam feeling the attraction for her that she'd experienced when she'd seen him. But he seemed distracted by Jenna's stepsister, Tansy, the short brunette who was staying out at Shadow Lake. Mallory knew Tansy didn't like her. She found her pushy and abrasive. Mallory was well aware of the other woman's reaction—it was her business to read people. And Mallory *had* been pushy. And then there was the little matter of Tansy not liking her because Tansy knew Mallory was interested in Liam. But that was too damn bad and not Mallory's problem because the stars had fated her and Liam. Liam was meant to be hers.

Her problem, professionally speaking, was in getting Liam Reinhardt to grant her an interview, to talk about his military career and experience. The man had summarily turned down a couple of interview requests—not from Mallory, but from other sources. As a military historian, she desperately wanted this interview with a man who arguably deserved to go down in history as one of the greats of his era in military sharpshooting. It was a shame that he had been discharged, but his experiences needed to be recorded for posterity and she wanted to be the one to do so. And yes, she could've called but she wanted to bask in his presence, to see the look in his eyes when he recognized what they could be to and for each other.

"Well, sometimes what we think we want isn't meant to be. You just have to let it play out."

Perhaps in some circumstances but not with them. Mallory *knew* she and Liam were meant to be.

She finally relaxed and let Ellie work her magic.

Mallory would simply show up on his doorstep. He couldn't ignore her—or their intertwined destinies—then.

LIAM WASN'T SURPRISED when Dirk slid into the seat opposite him at Gus's the following day. He'd known his and Dirk's business wasn't done, although there shouldn't be any more exchanges of blows. At least he hoped not. If there was a next time, Liam would hit back.

"How's your face?" Dirk said.

"Your face looks a whole helluva lot better." He'd lost the wild mountain-man face with a shave and a haircut.

Dirk laughed, looking more like the guy Liam knew. "Yeah. I didn't want to scare any of the little kids in town so I dropped by Curl's and he hooked me up. Your face okay?"

Liam ran his hand over his own chin. "Still intact."

Ruby, the pretty redhead, dropped by for their orders. She was attractive but she wasn't Wellington. They ordered and she left to get their drinks.

Dirk tilted his head to one side in inquiry. "So, what are you doing here?"

"I guess the same as you. Rolling." If anyone would understand aimless wandering, it was Dirk.

He nodded with acknowledgment. "How long you going to stay?"

"Hell if I know. I've got no plan, except to get out of bed every morning and who knows, I may decide to change that up." Liam wasn't into gambling, strip clubs or booze—three money drains for some guys—so he'd just socked away his cash each month. Financially, lying around in bed for a while was an option if that's what he wanted.

"Damn, skippy. That's a different song and dance for you."

"Life changes." And Liam didn't want to talk about his defunct career and lost sense of purpose. He was more than happy to talk about Dirk for a while. "How long are *you* staying?"

Ruby showed up with Liam's water and Dirk's beer. "The food'll be out in a minute."

Both men nodded and she left.

"I'm thinking I'll hang here for a while," Dirk said, picking up the conversational thread of how long he was hanging out in Good Riddance. "I've got some time off up on the pipeline and some dough tucked away.

If you're interested, I could probably get you on. The money's pretty good."

"I'll think about it." But it really held no interest for him. He figured when something struck him as right, he'd know it. "I'm good working construction with Sven for now. Look, since you slugged me over it, let's clear the air about Natalie. I didn't know I was poaching or I'd have never gone there. That's not my style."

Ruby placed a burger platter in front of each of them. "Anything else?"

Both Liam and Dirk shook their heads no. Liam continued. "If you still feel something for her, and you obviously do, you should look her up."

Dirk was suddenly fascinated with adding a small lake of catsup to his plate. Liam wasn't sure whether he planned to drown his fries or eat them. "She made her choice."

"Yeah, well, I obviously was the wrong choice."

Dirk glared at him across the table, as if he might take another swing. "Did you do right by her?"

Damn, but his cousin was hung up on Liam's ex-wife. That much was obvious. "If you were anyone else," Liam said, "I'd tell you it wasn't any of your damn business, but you seem to care about her so, yeah, I did as right by her as I knew how to do. I didn't screw around on her if that's what you mean. As far as I know, she didn't screw around on me."

"Natalie wouldn't," Dirk jumped in.

Damn. Dirk was definitely a head case over her. "No. She's not that kind of woman. She said she couldn't take me being gone all the time. It takes a different kind of woman to live those long stretches with her man gone. It just got to her, to us. She said I was married to the military first and her second." Liam shrugged. "She was right. She said she wanted to come first with her man. You should give her a call."

Dirk dredged a fry in catsup. "Did you ever think that you should give her a call now that you're out?"

"Nah, that ship has sailed for both of us," Liam said. "Damn, man, you care enough to knock me out in a room full of people and now you want to push me back into her life?" He shook his head. "That's some screwed up thinking."

The big man across the table scowled. "I just want her to be happy."

"Then give it a shot yourself, idiot."

Dirk turned a dull red. "I might look her up. We'll see. So, what happened that you're out?"

"I'm out of the military. It's the past so it just doesn't matter."

"I call bullshit on that. If it didn't matter then you'd talk about it. But, it's cool."

There wasn't much to say to that because Dirk was correct—it did matter, but he damn sure didn't plan to discuss it.

THE SOOTHING SOUND OF the waterfall in the reception area and flute music greeted Tansy as she walked into Jenna's spa late in the afternoon. The small reception desk in front of the waterfall was empty.

Ellie, her glossy black hair in its signature single braid, came down the hall. "Hi, Tansy. Are you looking for Jenna?"

"If she's not busy."

"She popped upstairs to check on Logan and Emma."

"Thanks." Tansy headed for the door marked Private. Jenna wouldn't care if Tansy dropped in for a few minutes.

She walked up and knocked on the door at the top of the stairs. "Come on in," Jenna sang out.

Tansy walked in. Jenna's home was beautiful. Huge windows let in light and offered awe-inspiring views of towering evergreens against a backdrop of distant snow-capped mountains and blue sky. Inside it was cozy and homey with a pink-and-yellow chintz sofa and love seat. A leather recliner added a masculine touch. A breakfast bar separated the den from the sunny kitchen.

Jenna sat curled up on the couch, Logan next to her. Jenna's blouse was unbuttoned and Emma nursed noisily, her dark head in contrast to her mother's pale breast. It was a sweet moment and a longing inside Tansy unfurled.

"Have a seat," Jenna said.

"I'm just on my way out," Logan said, rising.

"I don't want to interrupt."

"Seriously, you're not interrupting anything. Emma's still chowing down and Logan's on his way out."

"Bye, punkin. Keep your mama straight until Daddy can get back."

He dropped a kiss on Emma's head and then Jenna's forehead. As he headed out, he called, "See ya, Tansy."

"Bye, Logan."

The door had barely closed behind him when Jenna nodded, a big smile on her face. "You slept with him, didn't you?"

"Oh, God, don't tell me it's all over Good Riddance already."

"No. But it's just a matter of time. You've got that look about you...relaxed, kind of a glow...."

"Oh, please."

"What? Am I wrong?"

"Well, no...." Tansy laughed. "You're right. I don't know about glowing, but I do feel relaxed."

"I work with skin. Trust me, you're glowing."

"Well, I've got a bit of a dilemma."

"You need condoms."

"How did you know?"

"You came here brokenhearted. He came here pissed off. Neither one of you was likely to have been anticipating sex, so it stands to reason you need condoms and you don't want to go shopping over at the dry goods store for something like that." Jenna laughed. "Your mouth is hanging open."

"That's just plain scary."

"No. Just logical. I keep a big supply in the closet downstairs. So does Merilee. We like to keep the women in Good Riddance happy...and safe. However, we all know that condoms aren't one-hundred percent fail-safe, as little Ms. Emma is here." She giggled, much like she used to when she and Tansy were tweens and breaking in training bras and braces. "Thank goodness."

She transferred Emma to her shoulder and started patting the baby's back. "She is a cutie," Tansy said.

Emma issued a resounding burp. "And a delicate little thing, too," Jenna said with a proud-mama grin.

"Let me put her down for her nap and then we'll hook you up so you aren't having your own bundle of joy nine months from now."

Tansy laughed but it stirred all kinds of emotions inside her, not the least of which was a longing for what

Jenna, Logan and Emma had…and the realization that life was altogether too complicated.

But in the meantime, she and Liam would have a very good time.

LIAM SPOTTED HER THE MOMENT he rolled down the road. She was sitting on his porch step, obviously waiting. She'd parked a pickup—wonder who she'd borrowed that from—to the right of his cabin.

Mallory Kincaid, the sun glinting off of her blond hair, issued a small wave of greeting. He didn't wave back.

His first thought was they were about to get to the bottom of something. Obviously his instinct hadn't been off when he'd sensed her interest was beyond casual. His second thought was she was bold as he had neither encouraged her nor invited her. Close on the heels of all of that was the thought that he couldn't seem to get people to leave him the hell alone.

He parked his bike and walked toward her. He stopped short of the porch.

She stood, smiling. "Good afternoon."

"What do you want?" he said.

She looked slightly taken aback, but not intimidated. If anything, she appeared faintly amused. "That's blunt."

"I don't see the point in being otherwise." He wanted his swim, Tansy and dinner…and in that order. He didn't want an uninvited, unwelcome visitor. "What do you want, Ms. Kincaid?"

"Mallory. Please call me Mallory."

He ignored that. "I didn't invite you here. You've got

two minutes to tell me why you're here and then I'm going in that door. You can waste your two minutes on bullshit or you can state your case." He glanced at his watch. "Your two minutes start now."

She shrugged and nodded, as if accepting his terms. "I'm a military historian. My family has a long history of service that dates back to the Revolutionary War. My uncle served in Vietnam with Carlos Hathcock. My oldest brother was in Kosovo and Afghanistan. I want to document your contribution—"

"No."

"But—"

"No."

"It's important. And you're one of the greats."

He was not going to feed her curiosity and the curiosity of others as a "has-been." Four months ago, he would have talked. Now, she could get the hell out of his face.

"Your time is up." He walked past her and she turned, watching him. He paused at his door. Her two minutes were spent, but he had some questions of his own. "How did you know where I was?"

She shrugged. "It's not hard to find people."

"I don't like being stalked."

She shifted, leaning casually against the porch rail and post. "I don't consider it stalking. I consider it doing my job."

"Well, hopefully you can get a nice little vacation out of your time here. Otherwise you've wasted your time and your money tailing me."

She didn't bat an eye. "I don't give up easily."

"You're spinning your wheels and, as I said, I don't like being stalked."

"At least look at my work," she countered. "I'll do a great job of portraying your contribution without hyperbole or conjecture."

"Leave me alone." He enunciated clearly.

"An hour. I'm only asking for an hour." She raised her chin. "I'm going to write about you regardless because you're too important not to. You can either give me insight and the straight scoop or I'll do the best I can on my own."

That gave him pause. He didn't like being strong-armed but there was something to be said for making sure facts were presented correctly. And dammit, he could see it in her eyes. She fully intended to write about him. If she got it wrong, he could sue but that wasn't really his modus operandi and retractions didn't mean shit. What initially was in print was what people remembered. While he didn't particularly give a rat's ass what people thought, at least the record would be straight.

"I'll think about it."

"I leave in three days."

"I said I'd think about it."

She reached into her pocket and pulled out a business card. "My cell number is on there. You can search me on Google. I'm legit."

He took her card but didn't look at it. "I get final editing say-so."

"No." She shook her head as she delivered her immediate, firm denial. "That's censorship and I won't be censored. I suggest you check out my work online."

He felt a grudging admiration. She was ballsy and she wasn't backing down on her brave front.

He would think about it. He held her card up between two fingers. "I've got your number." He opened the door and stepped inside. "I expect you to be gone when I come back out."

She smiled. "I'm already on my way." She walked down the two steps. "I look forward to hearing from you."

Liam closed the door on her without replying. He had a lot to think about.

9

TANSY TURNED ONTO THE ROAD leading to Shadow Lake and was taken aback when she met another vehicle. Secluded and off-the-beaten-path in an area that was already remote, Shadow Lake got virtually no traffic. Mallory Kincaid waved from behind the wheel of a pickup truck.

Tansy returned the wave even though her gut somersaulted, a sense of betrayal washing over her. And then she realized it was a response that came from her experience with Bradley and this wasn't Bradley. This was Liam and she knew in her gut, deep inside her, that whatever business Mallory Kincaid had had with Liam it hadn't been monkey business. Liam had been in bed with Tansy last night and now Mallory had been out here, but she knew as surely as she knew her name he wouldn't have gone there. Some men just enjoyed the chase and once the hunt was over, it was on to other prey. She didn't have that sense with Liam. He might be abrupt and abrasive at times but he was a man who reeked of integrity.

And even though they were two ships passing in

the night, Tansy expected to be the only ship sharing docking space with him, even though they were short-term. The fact that she was so sure she was the only one docking with him was either a testimony to Liam or an indication that she was in fact recovering from Bradley's betrayal.

She'd seen Liam as a rebound, as a recovery from Bradley, but her feelings about Bradley were still all tangled up. She still hadn't really let go of the notion of them as a couple. She still had this little fantasy going in the back of her mind where Bradley showed up, full of contrition, vowing undying love and begging her to come back home to live happily ever after.

She parked and was walking toward her stairs when Liam stepped out onto the porch next door. "Did you see the Kincaid woman?"

Tansy hoped she managed to keep her expression neutral as she nodded. "I did."

He crossed the small yard to where she stood and rubbed his hand over his face. "She was waiting on my doorstep when I got home."

Well, hell. Tansy wasn't quite sure what to say to that. "Oh. Uh…that's different." She had struck Tansy as bold and well, that was bold. And she'd been right—Mallory was interested in him. Showing up on his doorstep was definitely interested. And all of that aside, there was something about the other woman that just raised the hair on the back of Tansy's neck. Tansy just got a weird vibe from Mallory.

"She wants an interview," Liam said.

That was so not what she'd expected. It took her a hot second to assimilate what he'd said. "An *interview?*"

"Yeah. She's a military historian and she wants to interview me about my time in the service."

Tansy's level of relief verged on the ridiculous. She couldn't stop the smile that bloomed on her face. "That's cool." Although why she'd had to fly all the way to Alaska and then into the backwoods for an interview was a question that begged asking. But hey...

Liam's scowl, however, clearly said he didn't find it cool. "I told her I'd think about it."

"Why not just say yes?"

He crossed his arms over his chest, his expression set. "Because it's done."

Together, they wandered up to her porch.

"Well, that's why it's history," she said. "I'm not sure I get your point."

"No, you wouldn't, would you?" He was as controlled as ever but the air practically vibrated with his frustration. "I'm a has-been. I didn't retire. I was medically discharged because of a faulty heart valve."

"Hold on a second. You run every morning and swim like that every evening and you've got a faulty heart valve?"

"I'm fine. It's fine. The doc said it wouldn't keep me from doing my job but since it's on record, it does technically keep me from doing my job, hence my discharge. Is that some bullshit or what?"

"Wow." She didn't even know what else to say.

"All I ever wanted to do was be in the military and now I don't have a damned thing to do." He squared his shoulders. "The only reason I'm thinking about letting her interview me is she said she would write about me one way or another."

"I don't see that you're a has-been. That implies that

you're all washed up." Tansy was just sort of thinking aloud.

"Do you see me in active service? Do you see me doing my thing? No. I'm carrying Sheetrock instead of a rifle. Do you have any idea how that feels?"

He wasn't the only one who found himself floundering professionally. "I hate to rain on your pity party but yeah, I kind of do have an idea of how that feels. I write a column that is carried all over the world, giving advice on love and relationships, and I'm working on my first book on finding your fairy-tale ending. Then I find out my fiancé was cheating on me. Do you have any idea how bogus that makes me feel? You haven't exactly cornered the market on professional and personal disappointment."

"It's not the same. No one took your column away from you."

"True, but then again, no one took your skills away from you. Just because you aren't in the service anymore doesn't mean you don't know your way around a rifle. Put it to use otherwise. There have to be other outlets."

"I'm not going to be a gun for hire."

"Who says you have to?" An idea popped into her head. "You're up here in Alaska. Why don't you do some wilderness training thing? You know, one of those survival camp deals? That would appeal to the kind of people who make Alaska their holiday destination."

Liam all but sneered at her idea. "Those that can, do. Those that can't, teach."

His outlook exasperated her. "Oh, really? Then it's a good thing that there are plenty that can't and teach what they can't do. That's some jackass thinking there, Reinhardt."

"What, Wellington? Are you thinking you'll change to career counseling since you're not doing so hot these days in the love department?"

She flinched inside, but remained outwardly poised. She knew enough about people to know he was striking out because he was so frustrated with his situation. It did not, however, mean she had to be his whipping boy. "That was uncalled for, Liam."

She used his first name deliberately, bringing the interaction back to a more personal level.

He looked somewhat contrite. "Yeah, I guess it was. Sorry."

It wasn't much in the way of an apology, but it was actually more than she'd expected from him. He obviously wasn't in a good place, which she fully recognized as she was sharing that same not-in-a-good-place designation. "No worries. But for the record, I think you should talk to Mallory—" even though Tansy still didn't much care for the woman "—and think about a survivalist skills camp."

"I'll think about it." And she had the impression that he would. "You keep writing your column and your book."

It felt like a peace offering for his earlier churlishness. She took it. "I will." She grinned. "It's how I pay my bills."

"Do you have any dinner plans?"

"No…" Was he actually asking her out?

"Want to make some dinner while I get my swim in?"

Really? He was serious. No teasing glimmer shone in his eyes. Yeah, she could make some dinner all right.

"I can make dinner *plans*—as in I can change clothes so you can take me to dinner at Gus's when you finish your swim."

He considered it for a couple of moments and then laughed. "Okay. You want to drive or you want to go on my bike?"

"I like your bike, but maybe I should drive."

He grinned. "Then I'll stop by in about an hour and a half. Does that work for you?"

"I'll be ready."

She had a date. It was a nice change.

Bradley who?

DAMN. NONE OF THIS WAS going according to plan. First, the Kincaid woman had been parked on his doorstep and then Tansy threw out the career idea and now they were going out to dinner. What had happened to his quiet home-cooked meal and hot sex afterward? Hell, he'd even sought out Bull after lunch to track down condoms. Thus was life in a town the size of a gnat on a map.

He supposed it was all good, except the Kincaid woman. Didn't anyone understand he didn't want his life delved into, that he simply wanted some privacy to lick his wounds? Apparently not. Although, it had been kind of nice to talk to Tansy about his situation. While she hadn't been particularly sympathetic, she had given him a different perspective. And, while they weren't in exactly the same situation, she did seem to understand.

The thought came out of left field that she at least got it in a way that Natalie wouldn't have. He and Natalie got along well and he'd loved and respected her and she'd seemed to feel the same about him, but he didn't think they'd ever really understood each other. Hindsight was twenty-twenty, but they would've been far better off just remaining friends than trying the husband-wife thing.

He knocked on Tansy's door. "Be there in a minute," she called out.

He waited, hearing her moving around inside. Finally she opened the door, looking fresh. A slight flush colored her face. She wore the same dress she'd had on at Gus's on Thursday evening. It looked as good on her now as it did then. "You look nice." He leaned in and kissed her cheek. Her skin was soft beneath his lips.

"Thanks. So do you."

He laughed at her handing it back to him. "Thanks."

She tilted her head to one side, perplexed. "What's so funny?"

"That you think I look nice. I trimmed my hair but my clothes choices were limited to my least worn jeans and T-shirt." He looked down at his jeans and boots. "I only brought what I could carry on the back of my bike. That's one thing you learn in the military—just take what you can't live without and pack light."

Her chin took on a stubborn tilt. "Well, I still maintain you look nice."

He grinned. "If you say so." He caught her hand in his. "Ready to head out? I'm starving."

Fifteen minutes later they walked into Gus's, Liam opening the door for Tansy and then ushering her to a booth with his hand resting slightly in the small of her back. More than a few looks came their way, some speculating, some smug. Merilee and Bull waved from across the room, where they sat at a full table.

He and Tansy had just placed their drink orders when

Mallory Kincaid approached their booth, speculation and perhaps a bit of consternation in her eyes. "Evening. Mind if I join you?"

Liam spoke up before Tansy could. In fact, he didn't even glance at Tansy. "Yes, we do mind."

Even the fairly unflappable Mallory Kincaid appeared somewhat taken aback. Her smile faltered and then she firmly pasted it back in place. "Uh, okay. See you later. Enjoy your dinner."

Tansy eyed him across the table as Mallory retreated. "That was blunt."

And her point was? "I am blunt. What? Did you want to have dinner with her?"

"Well, no."

"Okay. Neither did I. What's the problem?"

"You didn't even bother to ask me. Would it have mattered if I did?"

"Let me lay this out for you, Wellington. All day I've wanted to have dinner with you and then move beyond where we left off last night. Now, if I'd looked over to you for approval on her joining us for dinner, your sense of common courtesy would've kept you from saying you didn't want her to eat with us. So, then my and your private dinner would've been ruined. The only one at the table who would be happy with the situation would be her and I'm much more concerned with you getting what you want and me getting what I want. Dinner would've been spoiled and there was just no point in spoiling dinner for the sake of being polite. Somebody had to be in charge and I decided it was me. If you did want to eat with her, then you could always make arrangements to share a meal with her some other time, couldn't you?"

"That's true. However, next time I get to be in charge."

Liam laughed. "Fair enough." From the bar area, Dirk caught Liam's eye and pushed away, heading toward them. "Have at it. You're in charge."

It was a repeat of the Kincaid woman scenario. "Hey, slide over and I'll eat with you," Dirk said.

Liam kept his mouth shut and looked at Tansy.

She flashed Dirk such a warm, sunny smile that a twinge of jealousy bit Liam in the ass. "Maybe some other time. I want him all to myself tonight."

"Well, damn." Dirk looked at Liam. "You need to give me lessons, tiger."

Tansy laughed. She was damn sexy when she laughed. Actually, she was just flat-out sexy. "I think Ms. Kincaid was looking for a dinner companion."

"I'll see you later, then." Dirk headed toward the blonde.

"See?" She was cute even when she was smug. And he was suddenly extremely glad that she was being smug with him and not some other man. "There's blunt and then there's finesse."

Liam laughed. "That was well executed, but this was why I suggested you cook…unless you particularly want to have dinner with someone else. This place is like Grand Central."

Tansy shook her head, her dark hair swinging against her cheek. "It is Grand Central for Good Riddance. Why don't we have an appetizer here and get dinner to go?"

He trusted she'd meant it when she'd told Dirk she wanted him all to herself for the evening because he was damn sure finding himself unwilling to share her with anyone else. A bite or two would tide him over.

The woman across from him had main course…and dessert…written all over her. "That sounds like a plan."

"COME HERE," LIAM SAID, as she locked the front door and he placed the take-out containers on her kitchen counter.

A shiver ran through her. The glimmer in his eyes echoed how she felt.

"Are you in charge again?" she said. She actually found it pretty darn sexy.

"What do you think?" He leaned against the counter, looking hard, sexy, commanding.

"I think I might let you *think* you're in charge," she said as she slowly approached him.

"Are you trying to outmaneuver me with mind games?"

"Perish the thought." She stopped a foot away from him.

"Come here, woman." He pulled her to him.

"Hmm. I think I like it when you're in charge." She nuzzled against his neck. "It turns me on."

And it did.

"Keep your dress on. I wanted you the first time I saw you in it. Does that offend you?"

"No. It turns me on."

She felt as if she was on fire for him. It was as if all the other times, with Bradley, they'd had to build up to it. But with Liam, there was just this chemistry, as if when she was around him something crazy but real happened inside her. Him simply being him turned her on.

She ran her hand down the front of his pants and cupped the ridge of his erection. She rubbed her palm against the prize. "Unzip your pants. Does that offend you?"

"Not in the least." He unzipped.

She knelt in front of him and he groaned aloud. "It turns me on to have you on your knees in front of me."

Tansy licked the length of him from base to top and then took him in her mouth. She swirled her tongue around his shaft. The taste of him, the fullness of him in her mouth, excited her. Liam tangled his hands in her hair. She was so wet, so hot for him.

He gasped. "Enough."

He didn't have to say any more. She knew he was reaching his limit and he wanted the same thing she wanted. She wanted to feel his lovely cock inside her.

She rose and took his hand. "Bedroom." She'd left the bedside lamp on.

Liam quickly stripped out of his clothes, pushed her onto the bed, pulled her panties down and off and leaned back. "You're beautiful," he said as he rolled on a condom he took from his pocket. "Open yourself for me."

She touched herself and he shuddered. She spread herself for him and he entered her slowly. She savored the feel of him, inch by delicious inch. He was seated deep inside her and she tightened around him.

"Oh…" he gasped.

She wrapped her legs around him, pulling him deeper, harder into her. "Yes," she said.

He set up a slow rhythm of out and in and out and in. Tansy closed her eyes, letting herself go into the motion, the sensation. Liam pulled out of her and rolled to his back. "Your turn."

Tansy smiled and climbed on top. She settled onto his erection and sighed in pure pleasure, grinding down and around on him. She rode him facing him for a few minutes and then she turned her back to him and set up a thrust-and-retreat rhythm. Something in that hit just the right spot and she began to gasp as the beginning wave of an orgasm rolled through her. It seemed to resonate from somewhere deep inside her, with an intensity that left her spent and light-headed.

LIAM LAY ON HIS BACK and let the aftershocks quiver through him. Last night had been a relief and a release after a long period of celibacy, but tonight, this, her... She was incredible, felt incredible. He'd always enjoyed sex, but he'd never known it could be this good.

He drew her down to his chest to lie on top of him and pulled the cover over both of them. "Hmm." She snuggled in contentment against him, her head tucked in his shoulder, beneath his chin.

"When I can muster the strength to move, I'm going to take that dress off of you."

Tansy laughed softly against him. "Unless you just have some particular attachment to undressing me, I can take the dress off now."

"Hmm. Now would be good."

She shifted and wiggled and pulled the dress up and over her head.

"I can handle the rest."

She laughed. "The only thing left is my bra."

"Exactly. I can handle that."

Wrapping his arms around her, he unhooked her in the back. He slid the straps down her arms and took it off her. He realized it was the first time he'd seen her totally naked. Her skin was soft and smooth. Her breasts were full yet her nipples were a little on the small side, soft-pink eraser points atop her creamy mounds.

Liam teased one fingertip around the flat areola and felt her quiver. "Tired?" he asked.

"Content. You?"

"Satiated...but a little hungry."

"I'm glad to hear you say that, because I'm a lot hungry. I'm starving."

Liam chuckled. Most women wouldn't admit to having an appetite, especially a naked woman. It was refreshing. "How does dinner in bed sound to you?"

"Decadent. Fun. Satisfying."

"Wait...I think you've already skipped ahead to dessert."

"Shut up and get our food. And can you give me a T-shirt, second drawer on the right side?"

He levered out of bed, pulled out a T-shirt from the wardrobe and tossed it to her. "Thanks."

When Liam returned with the take-out boxes from Gus's, Tansy was sitting cross-legged against the pillows and headboard. He rather liked that she'd opted for that instead of putting her dress back on.

He passed Tansy a box and settled into the spot next to her.

"I think this is where we're supposed to exchange personal information," he said.

"You really don't ascribe to a whole lot of social skills, do you?" She opened the lid to reveal bison pot roast with mashed potatoes and green beans.

"Not particularly." He opened his container, as well.

"Well, for goodness' sake, I won't burden you with a lot of useless information about myself. God forbid that you might want to know something about me as a person and not just a convenient warm and willing female form who happens to be next door. There's nothing quite as gratifying for a woman as knowing she's merely a handy vagina." She took a bite of mashed potatoes.

"Why do I get the feeling I just said the wrong thing?"

"Ya think?"

"Let's try this again. Why don't you tell me about yourself?" The pot roast was delicious.

"Maybe it'll work better if you pretend it's a military interrogation and you ask what you want to know. I, however, reserve the right to not answer every question. I think we've already covered name, rank and serial number."

Liam laughed. "You and Jenna are stepsisters?"

"Yeah. Her mom and my dad got married when I was thirteen. My folks had been divorced for two years and I lived with my mom, but Jenna was there on my weekends and holidays when I was there to see my dad. We just sort of clicked. I had an older brother but I'd always wanted a sister, so it worked out even though things didn't work out between my dad and her mom."

"That's good that you and she stayed close even if things didn't work out with your folks."

"Jenna's mom is nice and she was always good to me, but she's either on her fifth or sixth husband. I can't keep up. It's like she's searching for something in someone else that she just can't find in herself."

"What about your mom? She remarry?"

"She's been in a long-term relationship. Mom left my dad because she finally came out of the closet. She's a lesbian. She and Dorothea have been together now for eighteen years."

He wasn't quite sure how he was supposed to respond to that. "Oh."

"It's all good. It was a bit of an adjustment at thirteen and kids at school can be really ignorant. Actually, people can be really ignorant in general, but you've just got to find the good things in life and let go of the rest."

Spoken like a true optimist. He wasn't sure anymore if he was capable of finding the good when the bad was so damn prevalent. "There's a whole lot of bad out there. Really, really bad. Sometimes finding the good is like looking for a needle in a haystack."

"I know you've seen a lot of bad."

"I've seen enough bad to last me a lifetime." And dammit, he'd been instrumental in stemming the bad, that had been part of his job and he'd be damned if he could find the good in the way that worked, in no longer being a part of the checks and balances out there.

"Then maybe that's why you're here now." Her comment tapped right into his head. "There are just some things that are outside of our control. What about your folks?"

"My dad died when we were kids. My mom never remarried. She's okay but she's difficult. She wants to manage everyone's life. I stay out of her business so she'll stay out of mine. I've got two brothers, a twin and a younger brother. And no, we're not identical. We all went into the military."

"And now you're starting a new phase of your life."

"It looks that way, doesn't it? What about your life? You came here for a bit, what happens next?"

"I came here to get some clarity and I guess accept that things didn't turn out the way I had thought they would. I thought Bradley and I were something we obviously weren't. I thought we had something we obviously didn't. So, I've regrouped. I know a lot of it is me, but in some ways, being here has made a huge difference. The town motto is something about leaving behind what ails you and it's true. There's something very healing about this place. I guess it sort of bears out the finding the good and letting the rest go."

"If you say so."

She laughed. "I just did."

10

TANSY FINISHED UP HER column and saved the file. She'd let it sit for a while and reread it before she submitted it via cyberspace. She'd never suffered these doubts as to the advice she doled out to others. But now she felt like a poser, a fraud, because, dammit, she was still so unsettled about Bradley and now Liam was on the scene. It had taken her all day to work through that column.

And she may not have her personal business in order, but she could at least maintain some semblance of order in her home away from home. She went into the kitchen and had just run hot water into the sink when her phone rang. It was Jenna's ring tone.

"Hey, you. How's it going?"

"Are you sitting down?" Jenna said.

Jenna didn't sound upset but Tansy's heart leaped into her throat. "Is something wrong?"

"No, no. Everyone's okay, but you might want to find a seat."

"Okay." Tansy crossed the room and sank onto the couch. It seemed the easiest thing to do. Her heart was thumping like mad in her chest. "I am now. What is it?"

"Bradley is here."

Tansy felt light-headed. She curled her fingers into the cushion, needing to grasp something, hold on to something. "Bradley? Here? In Good Riddance?"

"Yeah. Merilee just called me so I could give you the heads-up." Oh. Dear. God. "He's at the airstrip center and Petey's on his way to pick him up and take him out to you."

Petey, a part-time prospector and part-time mechanic, ran the "taxi service" in Good Riddance, which mostly meant he ferried people about in his Suburban for a token fee when needed.

Tansy sat, thankful for the sofa beneath her, stunned. Bradley was here. He had made the trip cross-country to see her. It wasn't as if he was just in the neighborhood and dropped by. He was here.

"Tansy?" Jenna cut into her reverie. "Are you there?"

"Yeah. I'm here."

"Are you okay?"

Oh, yeah, that was the question. She wasn't sure. "I think so. I don't know."

"Do you want me to come out? I can be there in a few minutes."

Jenna was a sweetheart but this was between Tansy and Bradley. Whatever was going to happen, whatever needed to be said, needed to happen with just the two of them. "No. No, I appreciate it, but I don't think so."

"Do you need to talk?"

"Not right now." She needed to pull herself together. "I need to organize my thoughts before he shows up, but I really, really appreciate the heads-up."

"Anytime. Call me if you need me. I'll keep my cell with me."

"I appreciate it."

"You'll call me after he leaves?"

Tansy laughed, as much from nervousness as amusement. "I'm sure you'll be hearing from me—probably before the taillights have faded. I'm going to run now."

She hung up and drew a deep breath. Forget about the dishes in the sink. Leaving the phone on the sofa, she hurried into the bathroom. While she rushed through brushing her teeth and hair and slapping on some makeup, her brain was running a thousand miles a minute.

She didn't know how she felt. Part of her wanted to see Bradley. Another part of her was dismayed. And what about Liam? Would he care? Would it make a difference?

She pulled on the much-worn dress, the one in shades of lavender, that she knew looked good on her, that played up her eyes. She had enough feminine pride that she wanted to "present" well. She hesitated and then defiantly pushed her glasses more firmly onto the bridge of her nose. Bradley had always preferred her wearing her contact lenses. She might put on the makeup and dress, but she was keeping the specs. Liam thought they were sexy.

She had just closed the door on her bedroom when she heard the sound of a vehicle coming down the drive. For all of her frantic thoughts and activity, a calmness descended over her. She sank onto the couch and waited. She wouldn't anticipate him at the door. He could knock…and wait.

The idea finally popped into her brain that she could actually refuse to see him. However, she didn't want him to think that she was afraid to see him or too vulnerable or still licking her wounds. No. She'd see him.

She heard his footfalls on the steps and then his knock on the door. Recognition rippled through her. The familiarity of his knock threw her for a loop, took her back to when they were an item. A sense of nostalgia and longing ripped through her. All the times she'd heard that knock before, all the good times that had followed. She shook her head, dispelling the memories. It was the past, water under the bridge. This was the here and now.

He knocked again, this time calling out, "Tansy?"

She didn't call out to him in return. Instead, she rose to her feet and crossed the room. Drawing a deep breath, she opened the door.

Bradley stood there...and she felt nothing. No anger. No wave of nostalgia. Just numb.

He motioned Petey to leave. Tansy motioned Petey to stay. He stayed, his motor running in the driveway.

"Hi, Tansy."

"Hello, Bradley." His sandy hair was short and well-groomed, as always. Uncertainty and contrition shadowed his blue eyes. There was a small spot on his cleft chin—she'd always found it rather endearing that he couldn't seem to shave without nicking himself there. Now, it was simply a thing—not endearing or otherwise. He wore a pair of pressed khakis and a collared light blue shirt—a combination she'd always found classy and sexy. He smelled like the Paco Rabanne he'd always favored and which she'd always found such an olfactory turn-on.

Now, it just was. He simply was.

Bradley shifted and she noted the Dockers on his

feet. He looked well put-together, albeit a little haggard around the eyes. He'd obviously taken the time to change before catching a ride out with Petey, considering he would've been traveling for a minimum of half a day, probably more.

"You look good. Alaska agrees with you."

"Thanks."

He shifted from one foot to another, as if unsure how to proceed. He looked beyond her, to the cabin's interior. "Aren't you going to invite me in?"

She hesitated and then made up her mind. She didn't want him in her cabin. She'd traveled more than a thousand miles to put herself in a place that didn't hold memories of him, of them. And she and Liam had been together here. "No. I'm not."

She reached behind her, stepped outside and closed the door.

"Ah. I see. You're not going to make this easy for me, are you?"

"It's not about making it easy or difficult for you. I simply don't want to invite you in." And that much was true. She didn't want him in her cabin.

He nodded, reaching out as if to touch her and then dropping his hand to his side. "You're still mad and I don't blame you."

It had been, still was, so much more than simply being mad. Try searing, soul-deep hurt, betrayal. And she didn't owe him any explanation and she certainly didn't care as to whether he faulted her for it. Tansy shrugged. "I don't care whether you do or don't."

A group of chickadees dive-bombed a feeder to the right of the porch and an eagle circled in the distance. A slight breeze teased her hair against her cheek. She stopped herself from wrapping her arms about her waist and instead kept her hands by her sides.

Bradley ran his hand over his head, his shoulders slumping forward. "Tansy, I know I hurt you. It was the most stupid thing I've ever done in my life." He looked deep into her eyes, as if he wanted to peer into her heart. She kept that door closed. "I've lived with regret and missed you like hell since you left."

She simply looked at him, a detached part of her noting that his eyes were nearly the same hue as the sky behind him.

He reached between them and took her hands in his, his fingers curling about hers. His touch, his skin, bore the familiarity of the hundreds of touches between them in their past. It shook her to her core. "I want you to come back with me. I want to fix things. I want us to get back to where we were."

She shook her head and disentangled her hands. She didn't care how it looked, she wrapped her arms about her middle. "There's no going back." It was a declaration as much for her as for him. "There's only moving forward."

He nodded eagerly, hope glimmering in his eyes. "Then let's move forward together. We'll see a couple's therapist. We'll work on it. You're the best thing that ever happened to me and I screwed up big-time."

She bit the edge of her tongue, just to make sure she was fully awake. It was nearly verbatim every grovel-and-beg-for-her-back fantasy she'd indulged in when they'd first split.

But this was no fantasy. This was real. Bradley was flesh-and-blood standing before her. Where was the sense of vindication she'd anticipated? Where was any sense of elation?

Despite her off-putting body language, Bradley wrapped his arms around her, pulling her to his chest. He pressed his cheek to the top of her head. It was hauntingly familiar...and disconcerting rather than comforting. "God, Tansy, I've missed you." He pulled back enough to stroke her jaw tenderly with his hand, his eyes drinking her in. "At least say you'll think about it. Will you at least give me that?"

She felt awkward and uncertain and a little trapped. And she heard the thrum of Liam's motorcycle at about the same time it appeared.

"I'll think about it," she said, trying to extricate herself from his embrace.

He, however, wasn't letting her go that easily—she supposed either figuratively or literally.

Liam killed his engine and climbed off of his bike. He walked toward the porch, a marked contrast to Bradley. Liam, in jeans, T-shirt and work boots, was dark and hard.

He looked Bradley over in cool appraisal and then looked away, clearly dismissing him. His eyes tangled with Tansy's. "I could use a back rub after my swim. I'll make dinner tonight."

Liam was definitely marking territory and drawing his own line in the sand. And she had no intention of changing her current plans, which had been to spend the evening with Liam, just because Bradley had shown up. And there was a big portion of her that was delighted that Bradley knew he wasn't the only game in town. "Okay."

Bradley's eyebrows drew into a straight line as he

frowned, looking between Tansy and Liam and then training his gaze on Liam.

"Who are you?" Bradley asked with more than a hint of belligerence.

Liam ignored Bradley. "Call me if you need me," he said as he turned on his heel and walked away.

Bradley looked back to Tansy. "Who is that guy? Obviously you haven't wasted any time." He had the nerve to look wounded.

Things should have been crystal clear, but Tansy had never felt quite as conflicted as she did at that moment.

When it was clear she had no intention of explaining Liam, Bradley continued. "I thought we'd have dinner together."

"I obviously have plans."

"What do you mean you have plans?"

"Just that. I have plans."

"Tansy, I flew across the country to see you."

"Bradley, I didn't ask you to come."

"Fair enough. I know I hurt you."

She nodded. He had hurt her.

He rubbed his hand over his brow. "Okay, I'll head back to the bed-and-breakfast and leave you to whoever he is, but will you at least sit down and talk to me while I'm here? I think we both owe it to ourselves and what we had to at least talk about it and try to work things out."

She hesitated, taking a minute to think. She didn't want to just send him away. She *couldn't* just send him away. She looked at his feet. "Did you bring some other shoes?"

He looked at her as if she'd lost her mind. "Yeah."

"Come back tomorrow at eleven. We can go for a hike and talk then."

For a second he looked as if he was going to argue with her. She didn't know whether it was the waiting until eleven or the hiking that he had issue with. She didn't care. He could come back at eleven and they could hike and talk or he could sit around and then go home. He wisely decided to roll with her plans—she saw it in his eyes. He nodded. "Okay. I'll be back at eleven." He glanced at the cabin next door. "Who is he? What is he to you?"

There were two issues here. One, she wasn't exactly sure what Liam Reinhardt was to her. Second, she didn't owe Bradley an explanation as to what Liam was to her—Bradley had forfeited the right to know when he'd cheated on her. The first question, however, was easy enough. "He's a former Marine sharpshooter, a sniper who is living next door."

"Oh. What is he to you?"

"That's private."

Bradley narrowed his eyes but nodded nonetheless. "We'll talk tomorrow."

LIAM ADDED A CAN OF TUNA to the pasta noodles and stirred it all together. It wasn't gourmet by a long shot, but it was dinner, after a fashion.

The Suburban had been gone by the time he'd gone out for his swim. Something had crawled over him, gone through him, when he'd driven up and seen—what was his name?—Bradley, with his arms around Tansy. He'd been a little disturbed and curious. It was like finding out the enemy had broached your perimeter. Although Bradley wasn't exactly the enemy. Tansy was simply a short-term thing, nothing more and nothing less which suited him just fine considering where his life was at this juncture. He was too unsettled and at a loss for her to be any more or any less.

He heard her door close and shortly thereafter her footfalls as she mounted his steps, then her knock. The first thing he noticed when he opened the door was that she'd changed into a pair of jeans and a T-shirt.

"Hey," she said.

"Hey, yourself," he said with a smile. He stood aside to let her in. Desire, hot and swift, flared inside him at the cling of her jeans to her hips and the way her T-shirt hugged her breasts. "You okay?"

She didn't pretend to misunderstand him. "Yeah. Still a little surprised, but I'm fine."

"You didn't know he was coming?"

Tansy's laughter held a note of incredulity. "Uh, no. We haven't kept in touch. I haven't heard from or seen Bradley in over a month."

"You still up for dinner?"

"A girl's got to eat." She smiled. "But maybe you could take a rain check on the back rub. And I'm not sure I'll be the best company."

"I can live without a back rub. And don't worry about whether you're good company or not. We'll just eat, okay?"

"It's a deal. Thanks."

"Have a seat and I'll dish it up. You may want to hold the thanks, though, because it's just stove-top tuna. It's one of only a couple of things I cook. My big criteria in the kitchen is quick, easy and some semblance of nutrition."

She sat down at the small kitchen table while he spooned up the food. "Water or milk?"

"Water, please."

Liam brought the food and drinks to the table and then settled in the chair across from her.

"Dig in."

"It's good. Kind of like comfort food. My mom used to make something similar when we were kids and she got in late from work."

"Glad you like it. So, was it a nice visit?"

"I can't say that it was nice. It just was. Is."

"I see. Is he sticking around for a while?"

"Jenna says he's here for two days. We're going for a hike tomorrow."

Liam nodded. "I'm guessing if he came all this way he wants you to go back with him."

"That's what he says."

"I see. I guess you've got some decisions to make."

She shrugged. "I guess I do."

"Just so you know, Wellington, I don't share."

"I didn't think you did. You don't strike me as that type. Neither do I, Reinhardt. I'll let you know if things change."

"Fair enough." He didn't want things to change. He wanted them to roll along the way they were until she left. He enjoyed her company and the sex was good, too…make that better than good. And there wasn't a whole helluva lot more to be said on that topic. "So, you never did say how you got started writing a column for the lovelorn."

"You never did ask."

"I'm asking now."

"It's really kind of crazy the way it all happened.

My degree is in art history with a minor in psychology. I know, they're not even remotely related. I always seemed to be the go-to girl when my girlfriends needed relationship advice and it always seemed to work out pretty good for them when they listened to me. It almost became something of a joke. As a lark, one of my friends set up a webpage and before I knew it, I went viral. Agnes, my friend who'd set up the page, suggested selling ads. Well, at that point we didn't have to sell anything because we were being approached by advertisers. I loved doing that a whole lot more than the job I had and I was being stretched pretty thin, keeping up with the website and my day job so I dumped the day job and started working the website full-time."

"You ever hear from people who say your advice sucked?"

"Occasionally. But it's mostly a case of people sometimes not wanting to hear what you have to say. The thing I love about it is I feel as if I make a positive difference in people's lives. Even if I tell them what they don't want to hear, it's really to get them to a healthier place."

"So you can really live anywhere. Work anywhere."

"As long as I've got an internet connection, I'm in business."

"That's a nice freedom."

"Yeah. I guess it is. I hadn't really thought about it. I always liked where I lived. But when my relationship with Bradley went down I came out here to get away for a while. Plus, I hadn't seen Emma yet."

"Do you miss…where is it…Chattanooga?"

"Not as much as I had thought I would. But it's one

thing to go away for a visit and a whole different ball game to think about moving for good."

"Yeah. I understand."

He got up and moved behind her. He put his hands on her shoulders and rubbed. "You're tense. Relax. I'll give you the back rub and you can catch me up another time. Deal?"

"That's a nice offer, but you know what I'd find much more relaxing?"

She caught his hand in hers and brought it to her mouth, pressing a kiss to his knuckles. Half an hour ago, he'd have turned her down, but then half an hour ago she wouldn't have made the offer because mentally she had been somewhere else, her mind wrapped up in her ex. Now, he didn't need to be asked twice.

"That works for me." He helped her to her feet and wrapped his arms around her, pulling her close, simply holding her for a moment. He kissed her, slow, deep, thoroughly, testing the weight of his lips against hers, discovering the recesses of her mouth, the texture of her tongue. He pulled away from her.

"Let's go to the bedroom." He didn't feel the franticness he'd felt before, last night and the night before. He wanted slow time with her.

"Okay."

They went into the bedroom and silently, of one accord, undressed. Unhurried. He pulled back the covers and they climbed into bed together. He touched her cheek, her neck, feeling the beat of her heart, the rush of her blood, beneath his fingertips. Still silent, she smoothed her hand over his jaw, palmed his chest.

He kissed the ridge of her collarbone, weighed the fullness of her breasts. He traced the darker circle of her areola and then teased his tongue against her ripe nipple. He lapped at her and then took the turgid point in his mouth and suckled as she plied her fingers through his hair and moaned in the back of her throat.

He kissed his way down her torso to the softness of her belly. He nuzzled at the curves of her hips.

"Liam." She spoke his name softly, almost a sigh.

He felt the fullness of her thighs, the firmness of her calves, and tested the delicate arches of her feet with his hands. Then he made his way back up to the soft, wet folds beneath the fullness of her bush.

He pulled on a condom and eased into her. She was beautiful, her dark head against his pillow, the softness overlying the steel that was her, welcoming him inside her. She draped her legs over his shoulders and he wrapped his hands around her thighs, going deeper, harder, as if he could get to the core of her, meld with her.

He felt her tense, felt the tightening of her around him. She fisted her hands in the sheets. He came with her, riding the orgasm that seemed to come from some place inside her, inside him.

_11_

THE NEXT DAY, TANSY GLANCED at the clock on her computer—almost eleven.

Despite dinner and the incredible time with Liam, which had rendered her beyond relaxed at the time, she hadn't slept worth a damn last night. If anything, the great sex with him had further complicated everything. She'd lain awake for what felt like all night, thoughts whirling through her head like a dervish.

She needed, wanted, some clarity but she was just as unsettled and confused as she had been. Actually, more so. Her plan, at this point after turning over both Liam and Bradley in her head all night, was just to hear Bradley out. She'd let him have his say and then figure it out from there.

It didn't mean he was in charge, but she was curious as to what was going on in his mind, his heart. She'd like to say she didn't care, but now that the shock and numbness had worn off, she did.

The sound of an engine coming closer heralded his arrival. The door slammed and the vehicle retreated as Bradley's footsteps reverberated on the porch steps.

Her heart tattooing against her ribs, she opened the door and stepped out onto the porch. "Morning," she said.

"Good morning." Even though his jeans and T-shirt were neat and pressed, he looked as if he hadn't slept any better than she had.

She found his haggardness gratifying. She had cried a veritable river over him, especially early on, so it was somewhat mollifying to see that he'd lost at least one night's sleep over her. She also found it slightly endearing.

"You ready?" she said.

"I don't even get invited in?"

No. She still wasn't ready for Bradley's energy in her space, even if it was a temporary space. That had been one of the reasons she'd come here in the first place. She'd move forward very cautiously. "I asked you to go for a hike, not sit in my den."

He wasn't particularly happy with her answer but he didn't have much recourse. He nodded. "Okay."

She walked down the porch steps and out into the bright day. Bradley followed her. The sun was warm against her skin. The light sparkled on the lake like diamonds scattered across its surface. The air, crisp and clean, sifted through the trees. Birds called to one another as if celebrating the day. At the end of the dirt path that led to Liam's cabin, Tansy hesitated.

Several trails ran through the property. The best-marked trail was the one she and Liam had taken the evening they'd spent at Juliette and Sven's place. It skirted the lake and offered stunning views of both the water and the mountains. However, she chose a more rugged path that ran perpendicular to that trail and led through the spruces to a clearing.

"This way," she said.

"You've become a regular nature girl, huh?" His laugh held a forced note.

Tansy didn't answer, letting the silence stretch between them as the towering evergreens filtered the sun to an arboreal twilight. She was giving him an audience, but it didn't mean she was going to make it easy for him. He didn't deserve an easy path, either figuratively or literally.

He stumbled over a root. "You're not going to make this easy, are you?"

The man did know her fairly well. "Life isn't fair or easy a lot of times, is it? I guess you make the most of whatever opportunity you find yourself given."

"I don't really know where to start."

She said nothing, continuing to put one foot in front of another. That had been all she'd been capable of when she'd first arrived here, simply putting one foot in front of another. Bradley would either find the words he wanted or he wouldn't.

The tall evergreens blocked the sun, save for the occasional shards of light that pierced the green canopy. The smell of his cologne struck a discordant note with the scent of fresh loamy earth and the trees. Ahead of them, the path and twilight gave way to a small opening of meadow. Tansy had often wondered what had occurred that nothing but grasses grew in the small space. She walked to the center and sank to the ground, wrapping her arms about her knees, the sun warm against her shoulders and back. Bradley lowered himself to sit beside her.

"This is beautiful. Remote but beautiful."

"I know."

He drew an audibly deep breath. "Okay, I screwed up. Actually, that's an understatement." *No kidding.* He paused and plunged on. "It was a couple of drinks and temporary insanity. That's no excuse, just what happened." He looked at her. "God, if I could go back and take it back I would but I can't. I've missed you like crazy." Real pain thickened his voice. "I've missed the sound of your voice—" he paused as if at a loss "—your head on the pillow next to mine in the morning, talking to you…just being with you."

His words resonated with her. She'd felt all of that herself. Some men weren't great communicators, but that had never been Bradley's problem. Words came easily to him. The fact that he was struggling now spoke volumes in and of itself. She didn't doubt his sincerity at all.

"Would you please, please say something?" he said, desperation echoing in his words.

She responded honestly. "I've missed you." And she had, dreadfully. He had haunted her days and nights… until she'd met Liam.

"God, that's a relief. I've missed you…been so lost without you. I was so scared…and then when I saw that guy yesterday. Damn, lambchop, I didn't sleep at all last night."

Guilt assaulted her. He *really* wouldn't have slept if he'd been a fly on the bedroom wall. She pushed aside the guilt. She and Bradley weren't an item anymore. He had torn that apart when he'd climbed into bed with that other woman. And he'd said it was a case of a few drinks and bad judgment.

"Are you saying it was just that one time?" she said.

"Does it matter?"

Did it matter? She wasn't sure. Either way it couldn't be undone. "I don't know."

"It was twice. I swear it was only twice."

It felt like a knife going through her. Twice with the same woman or twice under those circumstances? "The same woman?"

"God, yes."

She felt sick inside. So, it wasn't as if one night and one mistake had been their undoing. He'd seen her again, another time. "Okay."

"What does okay mean?"

It was funny how a sense of betrayal could uncoil inside you all over again. "Just that. Okay."

"So, this guy next door to you…you've slept with him?" There was no missing the edge to his voice. Good. Let him feel a little of what she was feeling, not that it was the same or even close to the same. She'd betrayed nothing when she'd slept with Liam because there'd been nothing to betray.

"Yes."

"More than once?"

She gave him back his earlier words. "Does it make a difference?"

"Then we're even," he said.

Tell her that hadn't just come out of his stupid mouth. "Really?" Outrage escalated her voice an octave. She swallowed hard and strove for her normal tone. "There's no 'even' to it. We're not engaged anymore." She held up her hand. "Do you see a ring on this finger?"

"That's why I'm here." He shifted, digging in his jeans pocket, and pulled out a small velvet-covered box.

He opened the top and the ring, her ring, sparkled in the sun. The night he'd proposed, the night he'd first shown her the ring, a symbol of promise, a declaration of love and fidelity and a lifetime of ever-after, the joy—it all rushed back at her and it all seemed little more than a mockery now. "Because this ring isn't on your finger and that's wrong." She determinedly looked away from the ring. It was just a thing. "I want to make things right. I want this ring back on that finger. I love you. I want us to fix things. I want us back together."

She stood, unable to sit any longer, a restlessness gripping her. She hadn't expected the ring. She looked down at him and absently noticed his bald spot on the top of his head had grown. She'd known it was there and it hadn't mattered. Ring still in hand, he rose to his feet.

"Put the ring away before you lose it," she said.

"If I put it on your finger then we'll both know where it is."

She shook her head. "Put it back in your pocket. I'm not sure that's what I want anymore."

"Shh. Don't say anything else right now." He did, however, close the box and return it to his pocket. "Tansy, will you at least think about it? I'm begging you to give me another chance."

She wavered. She didn't know if she had it in her to give him a second chance. However, she found that she just couldn't walk away from him. She didn't know what she wanted.

She spoke slowly, weighing her words. "I'll think about it. You've got to give me some time."

"Thank you." He pulled her close and inhaled. "I've missed the way you smell." He nuzzled down her face and murmured, "The way you taste." For the first time in what felt like a lifetime his mouth was on hers. He smoothed his hand over her hip and pulled her closer to him. There was no missing his erection against her.

She pushed away. "Bradley…"

He tried to pull her close again. "I want you, lambchop. In every way."

She stepped back, out of his reach. "I said I'd think about us, but we're not just picking back up where we left off."

"I know. It's just hard, lambie." She could attest to that firsthand. And she'd always loved it when he called her that pet name, but it was sort of working her nerves right now. "I've missed you." He stepped behind her and wrapped his arms around her, pulling her back hard against him. His breath brushed against her neck as he murmured in her ear. She had always loved it when he did that. "I could make you feel so good." He cupped her breasts in his hands. "Let me kiss your vajayjay. You know I know just the way you like it."

She grabbed his wrist and forcibly moved his hands, stepping away from him. "Whoa, whoa and whoa." She turned to face him, taking another step back for good measure, putting physical distance between them. "I don't know if I even want to kiss you again. The vajayjay isn't a remote possibility." Good grief, give the man an inch and he would take a mile. How he went from her thinking about forgiving him to cunnilingus was mind-boggling. And insulting.

"Ever?" He gave her his puppy-dog look. She used to find it endearing. Now it was just sort of annoying.

"Drop it, Bradley."

He threw up both hands in mock surrender. "Okay, okay. What about dinner tonight?"

She spoke without hesitation. "No."

"It's that Marine, isn't it?"

"Bradley, I answered all the questions about Liam that I plan to answer. And I was generous when I did that. You don't have any right to quiz me about anything."

"You're right. I just—" he ran his hand through his hair "—I can't stand to think… It makes me crazy."

She knew exactly how he felt as she'd lain awake her fair share of nights thinking of him in bed with someone else. He'd live. "You'll just have to deal with it."

"You've changed."

"I have, haven't I?" She was stronger, more sure of who she was. She and Bradley had been an item for so long, she'd been so young when they'd become a couple. Who she was had always been tied up in "them." She'd had to find who she was without him. "You say that like it's not a good thing."

"I don't know."

She realized with a start that it really didn't matter whether Bradley liked the new her or not. She liked her.

LIAM WALKED INTO Gus's and it seemed as if the conversations died at once, everyone turning to look at him. He looked back. It was just a few seconds and conversations resumed but it was a weird feeling.

Obviously everyone was busy speculating on what was happening between him and Tansy now that her fiancé had turned up.

Bull motioned Liam over to a corner booth. "You sitting down or is it a grab and go?"

"Grab and go. Sven's pushing to get this phase done so he sent me over to pick up lunch." Being the least seasoned on the crew when it came to construction meant Liam was essentially the gofer.

Over Bull's shoulder, Mallory Kincaid smiled a greeting that held an invitation. Liam acknowledged her with a slight nod and then turned his attention back to Bull. "That woman's a pain."

"She seems nice enough."

"She's pushy as hell."

"She's got a job to do and she wants to do it well." Liam shrugged at Bull's assessment. He had more immediate things on his mind. "You met Bradley?" Bull said.

"After a fashion. I saw him. I wasn't impressed. Tansy said he was coming back out today."

"He went. He's back in town now. Petey picked him up about fifteen minutes ago." Bull looked over Liam's shoulder. The hair on the back of Liam's neck stood at attention. "Speak of the devil... He just walked in from the B and B."

The room didn't come to a standstill, but a hush settled, voices lowering to a murmur. Liam didn't turn around. He knew all he needed to know about Bradley—he hadn't treated Tansy right. He'd hurt her. The guy was an asshole and Liam would be just as happy to smash his face as look at him, but this was Tansy's call.

"Approaching," Bull said, spotting for him.

"I know." Liam felt Bradley closing in on him. He kept his back to him. Around them, the room quieted once again. The only sound was a soap opera running on the wall-mounted television. And then someone muted that and the only sound was something frying in the open kitchen.

Bradley stopped and called him out. "Reinhardt."

Liam turned, looked the other man square in the eye and stared him down. "Yes?"

"I'm Tansy's fiancé." In one of those moments where life was stranger than fiction, Tansy walked through the door, stopping dead in her tracks at the sight of him and Bradley facing off. "Stay away from her," Bradley said.

"The way I understand it, you *used* to be her fiancé. And it's Tansy's call whether or not I stay away from here."

"I plan to marry her."

Liam smiled without humor. "Is that a fact? Once again, I think that's up to her."

Tansy stepped forward and spoke up. "First, don't talk about me as if I'm not even here. Second, have you both lost your minds?"

"Bradley started it. Liam was minding his own business," someone piped up from the back of the room.

Tansy glared at her ex. "Okay, so Bradley, you've clearly lost your mind."

He shook his head. "I'm lost without you."

Damn. This guy was a pathetic excuse of a man. What the hell had Tansy ever seen in him? Liam wasn't much when it came to love and romance, but even he could see this guy wasn't right for the General.

"Oh, brother," someone else said from another corner of the room.

Tansy covered her face with her hands and shook her head. She dropped her hands to her sides. "Oh, my God, this is like some bad soap opera or reality TV show."

"This is way better than a soap," said a tall man with red hair and a shock of red beard.

"Shut up, Rooster," someone called out.

"Which one do you want, Tansy?" Rooster asked. "We've got some bets going."

Bradley spoke, holding out his hand. "Tansy—"

She cut him off. "Do not say another word." He opened his mouth and she glared at him. "Nothing. Nada."

What the hell? He hadn't done anything but respond to the guy, but she seemed thoroughly put out with both of them, which he put down to general embarrassment that she was being publicly discussed. Oh, well.

And Bradley, spineless wonder that he was, turned tail and headed back over to the bed-and-breakfast. Meanwhile, Tansy marched across the room, head held high, back ramrod straight, to the counter. "I'd like whatever today's special is. To go."

The waitress nodded. "Sure thing." She looked over at Liam and called out, "Your order is ready."

Liam crossed the room, heedless of the looks being thrown his way. Behind him, Bull called out, "Turn the TV back on."

At the pick-up counter Tansy ignored him. Giving her space seemed a wise tactic. Liam picked up the cardboard box containing the crew's lunch and silently left.

Sometimes the wisest course of action was retreat. It did not escape his attention, however, that Tansy had left the question of who she wanted unanswered.

"HOLY MOLY," JENNA SAID, shaking her head from behind the reception desk in the spa lobby as Tansy closed the door behind her.

Jenna had obviously already heard about the spectacle that had just played out. "Okay, that was fast, even for Good Riddance. I came straight here from Gus's."

She'd covered the distance from Gus's to Jenna's spa in about five minutes, seriously needing to talk to her sister.

"Alberta was texting me from the restaurant," Jenna said, stepping from behind the desk and hugging her.

Tansy hugged back and then shook her head, still feeling as if she'd just had some out-of-body experience. "Jenna, it was surreal."

Jenna nodded. "Kind of bizarre, too."

Uh, well, that's what surreal was but Tansy just kept it to herself. Jenna was a genius at business but sometimes in other areas…

Jenna slid her arm around Tansy's waist, as if sensing her sister was still in some kind of oh-hell-did-that-really-just-happen shock. "I've got ten minutes before Rachelle Richardson comes in for a set of nails. Ellie's in the massage room and they can't hear." She led her to the nail area. "We can talk over here."

Tansy sat in the seat across from Jenna, the small nail table between them. She recounted the walk in the woods with Bradley…down to the nitty-gritty details.

Jenna's mouth dropped open and she leaned across the table, lowering her voice even though she'd reassured Tansy there was no one around to overhear them. "You mean he offered to go down on you in the woods?" Jenna's blue eyes were as big as saucers. "Like he just rolled into town and said—"

"Uh-huh. Unbelievable." It was funny how a little distance and a different man had given her a whole new perspective. She'd been so wrapped up in Bradley as an ideal that she hadn't seen him clearly before. Her Prince Charming wasn't so charming after all.

"Seriously?"

"Yep."

"And you said no?"

Tansy laughed and shook her head at Jenna. "Jenna…"

"Well, I'm just saying you could have…"

Tansy grabbed her head with both hands. "I feel like flushing my head down a toilet. I don't know what I want anymore. Maybe somewhere inside, all this time I've been hating on him, I've wanted him to do exactly what he's doing now—well, show up that is, not make a scene in Gus's. I don't know. In a way, I moved on, but I think some part of me was waiting for him. I wanted him to come for me the way Logan came after you. I thought that's what I wanted. But somewhere along the way, without realizing it, I did move on."

"Liam?"

"He was definitely part of it. But it's me. Bradley said today that I've changed and I have."

Jenna pursed her lips. "So, what are you going to do?" She leaned in, her eyes sparkling with excitement as if she'd just had a great idea. "Are you going to sleep with both of them? Sort of a test run at the same time?"

Both exasperated and amused, Tansy laughed. "Jenna, I swear. You won an award for probably the oldest virgin in the state of Alaska when you finally slept with Logan, but now, girl, you are sex-crazy."

Her sister's grin was infectious. "It's fun. It feels good. At least it does with Logan. I wouldn't know about anyone else but that's okay because if it was any better than it is with us, I think I'd probably just expire from satisfaction and Emma needs her mommy." Jenna rubbed her hands together. "So, are you? Boy Toy One and Boy Toy Two test-drives?"

"As much as I hate to disappoint your lascivious little soul, no I'm not going to test-drive them. And they're both too old or I'm too young, but whichever way you look at it they're not boy toys."

"All right, already. So, what's the plan? Because failing to plan is planning to fail."

"My plan is to take a break from them so I can think."

"Exactly what do you mean take a break? Not have any contact with them?"

"Well, I'm definitely not going to sleep with either one of them right now. Sex won't do a thing but muddy the waters for me and I'm not sure if I even want to sit down and have dinner with either one of them. When I'm with one, the other is just going to be hovering in the background—I mean that figuratively, but Good Riddance is so small, it'd be literally, as well."

"What has Liam said about Bradley being here?"

"He really only had one thing to say last night."

"Which was?"

"He doesn't share. And I know what he means because he and I are casual, but I don't share, either."

"Are the two of you casual?"

"Of course. We haven't known each other very long. We just fell into a thing. I think we were both convenient for each other at the time."

"Maybe or maybe not. Maybe it's always been more than just that or maybe it started out as just that but has changed."

"I don't know. I can't even think about it right now."

Jenna laughed. "I beg to differ. I think it's exactly part of everything you have to think about right now."

"This is all so complicated. How is it that you think

you know what you want, and then when it happens, you're just not sure if it's really what you want? I know Bradley and I can never go back to what we had and that's a good thing because there were holes in our relationship that I didn't see before. But now I don't know if I want to move forward with him, either. And it's really not an either-or situation with Liam or Bradley. Just because I do or don't want Bradley doesn't mean I do or don't want Liam. That sounds so convoluted. Do you know what I mean?"

"Hey, those are the conversations I'm best at following. I know just what you mean. Maybe you don't want either one of them eating crackers in your bed."

Jenna had a unique way of putting things. "Exactly."

"So, maybe just because you don't want Liam, it doesn't mean that you do want Bradley, or vice versa. Do you still love Bradley?"

Did she love him? He'd been a part of her life for so long that while she'd hated him at first, she'd found some healing in time and this place. "I don't hate him. I don't still wish terrible things on him like I did at first. But I'm not sure if I'm still in love with him."

"How do you think he really feels? Could you ever trust him again? If you can't trust someone, you don't really have anything."

"I do think he loves me and that's not just wishful thinking on my part. But one thing I've figured out is that the other woman…that was about him, not me. I know it took a lot for him to come here and I do think he's desperate to have me back, otherwise he wouldn't have made that scene today with Liam in Gus's. And Liam… I just don't know. I don't know about any of it."

"Well, the good thing is, you don't have to make a

decision now or even today. You don't have to make a decision until you're ready."

"That's true enough. It's up to me to decide, but I do know I don't want to drag this out. For me, not knowing is always worse than making a decision or finding out one way or another and then dealing with those consequences. Plus, Bradley is going to be pinging around like a loose cannon until I give him something, one way or the other. It was mortifying to have him and Liam discussing me in public today." She wrapped her hands around one knee and rocked back and forth. "What was it like when Logan showed up here, after all that time?"

"I knew inside the moment I saw him even though I tried to deny it. It's funny. I still feel that rush when he walks into the room. It's not as intense as it used to be, but it's real and it's there. I think the rush will always be a part of me, of us."

Tansy nodded, intuitively knowing exactly what Jenna was talking about. She'd felt the same thing… the first time she'd seen Liam Reinhardt.

12

THE FOLLOWING AFTERNOON, Liam decided to forgo his ritual after-work swim in lieu of a visit with Bull. He hadn't seen hide nor hair of Tansy since she'd ignored him in Gus's yesterday, which wasn't surprising. The woman had a lot on her mind. So did he. The crazy, disturbing thing was he'd actually missed Wellington last night. What the hell was up with that?

He parked his bike in front of Bull's hardware store and went in. The metallic smell of tools and the sweet scent of sawdust greeted him. Bull sat on the other side of the counter whittling.

"Got a minute?" Liam said.

"Got lots of them," Bull said, working the wood chunk, which had yet to take on any particular shape. It sort of seemed symbolic of Liam's future, which was why he was here now. "What's on your mind?"

Liam leaned against the counter. "I wanted to run an idea by you."

"Sure thing." Seemingly focused on the wood and knife in his hands, his uncle waited.

"I've been thinking about something Tansy mentioned the other day. She suggested a survivalist training camp since I have a special ops background. She said this area invited that kind of person in the first place. The more I think about it, the more I think it might work." Bull nodded and Liam continued. "I appreciate Sven hiring me on but I can't see me doing that for more than a season. And dammit, I've got to do something." He pushed away from the counter and gave voice to the frustration that ate at him, that had been eating at him since he'd been handed his discharge papers. "I'm thirty-one years old and wondering what to do with my life now that I don't belong in the military anymore."

Bull whittled on.

Liam continued, "I had it all planned, but with that discharge... What the hell. I don't know what to do with myself."

"Life has a way of doing that." He stilled his knife and looked at Liam. "I was eighteen and had all kinds of plans...then I was drafted to go to Vietnam. That didn't quite go according to plan, either. I just wanted to do my rotation and get back home." He pointed to the scar on his neck with the knife's point. "It didn't quite work out that way and when I finally got back, all those plans I'd had before just didn't fit. So, yeah, sometimes you've got to punt on the goal line. I know your frustration."

"I've just been pissed...so pissed I don't know what to do with myself...and I didn't have the experience you did. How'd you handle it?"

Bull folded the knife and crossed his hands on his still-flat belly. "I went around angry for a long, long time until I finally figured out that wasn't getting me anywhere. Plus, I met Merilee and knew she was the damn best thing I'd ever come across. Finally figured out if all that other shit hadn't happened, I wouldn't have wound up meeting her, so maybe I should be glad for all the crap that came before because I sure as hell am glad for her. She's the best thing to ever happen to my life, bar none. Once I started looking at it that way, I could let the other stuff go."

He had a whole lot of respect for Bull but that struck Liam as some faulty logic. "But maybe you'd have met her if all the other stuff hadn't happened."

"Maybe. Maybe not. I'll never know because it did happen and it was the reason I wound up here and I met her here so, there you have it. Sometimes it's damn hard to see a door opening in your life because you're so pissed over the one that just slammed shut on you and caught you in the ass and hurt like hell while it was closing."

Liam wasn't convinced. "I suppose."

"You've got to open your mind to possibilities."

"I guess I'm getting there since I'm having this conversation with you. I've been so angry, all I could think about was how angry I was."

Bull grinned. "Tell me something I didn't know. Your mom thought you were coming here to heal. I called bullshit on that the second I saw your face. You just came here to wallow in the shit you found yourself in."

Liam winced. "Guilty as charged."

"Nothing to feel guilty about. But I'm glad to see you're ready to quit wallowing and get on with life. The survivalist camp is a good idea. With your reputation,

I think you could be booking out a training camp and having people on a waiting list."

Excitement stirred in Liam in response to Bull's enthusiasm. Bull wasn't a man given to hyperbole.

Liam had been turning the logistics over in his head. "I'd need a big tract of land that would still be close enough to transport participants and supplies."

"If there's one thing we've got up here, it's land," Bull said with a grin. "You might find yourself with fairly primitive conditions, but land isn't a problem."

He'd done primitive. Hell, he'd sat out the enemy for days at a time without any provisions. "If it's survivalist training, no one should expect the Hilton."

Bull grinned. "Have you given any thought to bringing someone in with you on the operation? You're going to need a second-in-command."

"I'd need some help, but I haven't gotten that far. I just wanted to toss it around with you first."

"Can I make a suggestion?"

"That's why I'm here."

"Dirk."

Instinctively Liam rubbed his hand over his jaw. "What about him?" Surely, Bull wasn't thinking…

"You should bring him in with you on this."

"Dirk's a loose cannon. He knocked the hell out of me."

"Yeah and then he helped you up and you guys were okay. I know Dirk's always been a rolling stone but that's because he's got all the qualities of a second-in-command. He's just been looking for a commander and a spot he fits in."

Right off the top of his head, he wasn't seeing it,

nonetheless he respected Bull and his opinions. "I'll think about it."

"Just turn it over in your head a bit. Now, what about Tansy?"

"Wellington as part of my crew?" Damn, if Bull wasn't stretching the bounds of rationality there.

Bull chuckled. "No, Tansy just as Tansy."

"She's an interesting woman."

Bull stood and clapped him on the back. "You may be surprised at all the doors you find opening."

TANSY LEVERED HERSELF up off the couch. She was tired of her own head and her own company. She'd done nothing but think, think and think some more. Jenna had kept her updated on what Bradley had spent his day doing—warming a seat at Gus's, shooting a few games of pool and nursing beers. He'd called and texted. She wasn't being a bitch, but she needed some time away from him to think, which was ironic considering she'd had a couple of months away from him. But this was different thinking. He was just a few minutes away. And he wanted her to go back with him. And she wanted to think about something else. She wanted a distraction.

Night had settled around the cabin and over the lake. An owl hooted in the distance. Farther away still, a wolf howled. Within a few minutes another wolf answered. The scent of woodsmoke drifted in on the night air. She wandered outside and around the back of the cabin.

Liam sat near a fire pit where wood snapped and popped, casting an orange glow. A mat on the ground held various pieces of what looked like a rifle. He glanced over as she approached.

"Hi," she said. "Are you up for some company or are you enjoying your solitude?"

"Company is fine. Have a seat."

Tansy settled on a log to his right. It wasn't exactly cold, but the autumn nights had grown chilly and Tansy welcomed the fire's warmth. She hugged her arms to her knees and watched as he deftly cleaned the part in his hand. He had nice hands. Strong, capable. Sexy. Her body hummed, remembering the feel of them against her, gripping her thighs, testing the weight of her breasts.

"You have enough light to do that?" she said.

"I could do this in the dark blindfolded."

"Ah." She shifted. "I'm sorry about...well, yesterday at Gus's."

"You don't owe me an apology because you didn't do anything."

She had been angry at finding them discussing her but in retrospect, she realized Liam had simply been in the wrong place at the wrong time. Bradley had been the one who made her business public. Given his privacy issues, Liam had probably found it as embarrassing as she had, perhaps more so. "Bradley was—"

"You're not responsible for him. You didn't do anything so you don't owe me an apology."

"Okay. Nice fire. Reminds me of when I was a Girl Scout. You don't have any s'mores fixings, do you?"

His teeth flashed in the firelight. "Fresh out. So, you were a Girl Scout?"

"Of course."

"I bet you sold a lot of cookies."

"My fair share. Were you a Boy Scout?" She wasn't seeing it.

"Nope. That just wasn't my thing."

"I didn't think so, but I thought I'd ask anyway."

"We were too busy playing in the woods, hunting and fishing."

They exchanged tales of childhood misdemeanors, silly stories that made each other laugh. It was quiet and relaxed. There was something comfortable about his voice, the warmth of the fire and the night's darkness. They talked about a little bit of everything and a lot of nothing but it was nice.

"Do you want to go inside?" he said.

"No. I just wanted to share the campfire and some conversation."

"I understand." He hesitated. "I don't want to be presumptuous, but don't make any decisions based on me, Tansy. I'm trying to figure out my life. I don't have anything for anyone right now."

"I'm not." And she wasn't. "This is between me and Bradley, which is why I don't want to cloud the water with anything else." For all of his gruffness, abruptness and lack of adherence to social dictates, he really was a very nice man. "Can I ask you a very personal question, and it's really none of my business, so feel free to tell me to mind my own business."

"Ask and I reserve the right to not answer."

"Were you faithful to your wife?" The question hung in the night air and she found herself holding her breath as to whether he'd answer.

He did. "Yes. There was never another woman. There was my career and long separations, but there was no one else. I'm a man of my word."

She was somewhat surprised he'd answered. However, his answer itself didn't surprise her. It simply confirmed what she'd thought of him and his character. "That's what I thought. Thanks for answering."

"You'll figure it out, Wellington. I have great faith in you."

There was nothing left to figure out. She had all the answers she needed.

MALLORY CLICKED HER TAPE recorder to the Off position on the kitchen table. "Thank you."

Liam had left it down to the wire but he'd finally contacted her and granted an interview. She'd extended her stay. She'd known that day that she'd left his cabin that he'd come around, if for no other reason than to make sure she got her facts straight. But there was so much more to it than that. He had to have finally tuned in to this cosmic connection between the two of them. Her inner self was so tuned in to him, he *had to be* equally tuned in to her.

They'd arranged for her to come out to his cabin. He'd said it was simply for the sake of the interview not being interrupted. The only other real choice had been her room at the bed-and-breakfast and that didn't really work. There were a few tables that overlooked the main street in the front of the airstrip office, but that place had a steady flow of people coming and going so that had been out. Mallory, however, was certain he'd simply wanted the time alone with her, to get to know her better.

And now the business portion was finished—he was the kind of man who'd always take care of business before pleasure. They'd spent a couple of hours on the interview.

She'd dressed carefully, wanting to look professional

but also wanting to strike a feminine, alluring note. She packed away her notes and the recorder. She'd been in love with him from before she ever met him face-to-face here. Her friend Yvonne had dared to tell Mallory she was obsessed. Mallory, however, had known she'd found her soul mate. She and Yvonne were no longer friends. Just as she'd known he'd be, Liam, in person, was even more potent than on the video she'd seen, and the dry facts in his personnel file and other records hadn't done him justice, either.

"Can I buy you dinner?" she said as she stood to leave.

A perplexed frown furrowed his brow. "I thought you got all the information you needed."

Ah, he wanted to play a game with her, because him not being attracted to her simply wasn't an option. One of her girlfriends had told her once that she was pretty without being so gorgeous that she scared men off. It seemed to be true enough because sitting at home on a weekend night wasn't an issue. However, most men bored her. As a military historian, she dealt with men who were larger than life. Heroes. Most ordinary men simply couldn't measure up. Her last love interest had been a retired lieutenant colonel in his fifties. There was something about that combination of authority and power that did it for her. Liam Reinhardt was a man of incredible skill, valor, and he was damn hot to boot. Her man.

She was used to going for what she wanted. If you didn't ask, if you didn't throw the line out there, you didn't get. She cast her line. And this wasn't simply want—this was destiny. "This isn't business. You're very attractive, and one of the most fascinating men I've ever met."

He paused and she found herself holding her breath. "I'm flattered—" that foreshadowed a big old *but* "—and you're very pretty, but I'm going to pass. It's been a long day and I just want to kick back."

What? She couldn't just give up on them, on the future she *knew* they were meant to have together.

"I totally understand kicking back. I'd be glad to bring over takeout or I make a mean spaghetti sauce."

She saw it in his eyes before he even opened his mouth. "Thanks, but no."

No. No? It was that Wellington bitch next door. She'd clouded Liam's thinking, his perception. Mallory was for him. She recognized what a hero he was. She loved him, dammit. She was what he needed, not Tansy Wellington.

Mallory wanted to cry and kick and scream. Instead, she nodded. "I'll be in touch then if I find I missed anything."

And that was that...for now.

TANSY WALKED INTO THE airstrip office. Alberta had a tarot-card reading going over in the corner with a tourist. Dwight, Lord Byron and Jefferson were all huddled around the chessboard. Merilee and Dalton Saunders, the other bush pilot, were going over a schedule.

Merilee looked across the room to Tansy. "He's out of here in two hours."

"I know."

Merilee nodded. "Room three. All the way at the other end of the hall, next to the bathroom."

Tansy mounted the stairs. She'd slept on it, waited

until the last minute, had searched her heart one last time before she drove over here. She walked down the hall, her shoes echoing on the wood floor. She knocked. Bradley opened the door. "Come on in."

He looked terrible. There was a time, when she was so angry at his betrayal, she would've been near gleeful. Now she simply felt sad.

"Dammit, Tansy," he said, tears gathering in his eyes.

She didn't even have to say it. He saw it in her eyes, on her face. "It's just no use, Bradley. I care about you, but I just can't… It's not going to work."

"So does that mean you never loved me? Because if you loved me, you could forgive me. Is this just your way of punishing me?"

She shook her head. "This has nothing to do with punishing you. It told me something about the man you are and something about the woman I am and you're right, it did change me. I can't regret it because I grew from it. It was definitely growing pains, but growth nonetheless. So, we're not the same people we were and the people we've become don't belong together. It's time for both of us to move on."

She wrapped her arms around him and kissed him softly on the cheek. "Thank you for coming, Bradley. You set me free. I was stuck and you've unstuck me."

Tansy could see it in his eyes. He didn't get it, not even a little bit, which was even further proof that the two of them didn't belong together, not that she doubted it.

He grabbed her wrist, but not too tightly. "It's that Marine, isn't it?"

"No. How I feel about you has nothing to do with Liam."

"If I had gotten here a week before him—"

"It wouldn't have made any difference. This is about you and me, not me and him. It wasn't an either-or situation. And you and me aren't going to work."

That particular lightbulb still wasn't going off for him, but it really didn't matter. She'd said what she had to say and it was time for them to permanently part ways.

"Travel safe, Bradley. I wish you well."

"Yeah, right."

She simply shook her head as she closed the door behind her. Now she had one more piece of business to set in order.

She went downstairs and cut through the connecting door to Gus's. She really, really wasn't into making her life a public spectacle but within no time everyone would know Bradley had left without her and she wanted to make one point clear.

She made her way to where Rooster was sitting. As far as she could tell, Rooster's main income stream was operating as the local bookie. Rooster took bets on anything and everything and people placed bets on anything and everything. Some places had dog-track racing, some places had horse racing, Good Riddance just had the ins and outs of life that they bet on.

Norris, a retired newspaper reporter, and her boyfriend, a short man whose name Tansy never could remember, were sitting at the table with Rooster. Good, they could vouch for the information. "Hello—" she didn't see any point in beating around the bush "—I know there are bets placed and soon enough it'll go around that Bradley is leaving alone. I need to clarify that just because I didn't choose Bradley, I haven't chosen Liam, either."

"Let me get this straight 'cause it makes a difference in how the bets are paid out. You didn't choose Bradley and you didn't choose Liam. You didn't choose either one of them. Got it." He looked beyond Tansy's shoulder. "You got it?"

Tansy knew before she turned, before she heard the voice.

"Got it," Liam said.

Well, that was one way for him to find out.

13

LIAM FINISHED UP HIS NOTES and supply list with a renewed sense of purpose. He didn't still feel so angry that he couldn't think anymore. Talking to Mallory Kincaid had ultimately been a good thing, even though he'd been getting a kind of weird vibe from her, especially after the interview. The interview, however, had been a good thing.

He'd gained a perspective on his time in the military. It was the past, just like his marriage was the past. He'd always been so sure that a career in the military was his destiny, was where he belonged. And if he went with Bull's philosophy, that clearly was the case. So, he could go around being angry at the world and the unfairness of life or he could regroup. Nope. Life wasn't particularly fair. There wasn't a damned thing fair about life as far as he could tell. He'd seen too much of it to be that naive—there was no equity in the way some of the villagers lived in Iraq and Afghanistan. There was no equity in the way some Americans lived. What had been fair about Bull being a POW for two years? What had been fair in guys losing body parts to roadside bombs and living as half men? Nope. He could safely say fair wasn't part of life.

He could also safely say that he didn't have any control over having been kicked out—okay, discharged on a medical—but the thing he could control was what he did from this point out. He could sit around in his own crap, stinking up himself and the world, or he could get up, clean up and move forward.

That interview with Kincaid felt like moving forward. Making plans for his future, finding a purpose, felt like moving forward. He'd talked to Bull and was moving forward on exploring setting up a camp. He'd spent some time looking over topographical maps and he'd scheduled a reconnaissance flyover for tomorrow.

He picked up the two-way handset and "rang" Tansy next door.

"Wellington, how's your schedule looking day after tomorrow? Want to take a trip?"

"What kind of trip and for how long?"

"Just a couple of days. We'd be gone two nights and it'd be camping with no facilities. Just thought I'd ask, but no problem if it's not your thing."

"Keep talking. You've got my interest."

"I'm going to go look at a piece of property for that survivalist camp you mentioned. Either Dalton or Juliette will fly me in. I'll take a couple of days to hike around and get a feel for the terrain and then they'll pick me up a couple of days later."

"I see. So, like no running water, no toilets, no beds."

"A stream runs through the property. I'll pack a latrine shovel. And there will be a tent and sleeping bags with bedrolls under them. Gourmet freeze-dried rations. Deluxe accommodations."

"What about snakes and bears and other wildlife?"

"All possible. Fairly probable, in fact."

"What if something happens or there's an emergency?"

"We radio base and they fly in and pick us up. You ever been camping before?"

"Hel-lo. Remember, I was a Girl Scout. All Girl Scouts go camping at one time or another. We stayed in these little teepee things with platforms for our sleeping bags."

"Bathroom and showers?"

"Not in the teepees. We had to walk to get there and all the showers were in a row."

"But you've never done any wilderness camping?"

"Well, not exactly."

She'd be perfect. If she could do this, then greenhorns could. She'd be a good barometer. "You need to know, though, that if you go I'm not going to babysit you. You have to carry your own gear and keep up."

"When do we go?"

"Day after tomorrow."

She swallowed. "Okay. What do I need to do to get ready?"

"I'll pull together your gear. You put together some clothes and I'll look them over. Remember, you've got to carry everything on your back. How about I come over tomorrow evening and sign off on your clothes."

"I'll see you then."

"Are you going to feed me or do I need to bring dinner from Gus's?"

"I'll feed you."

"One more thing, Wellington. Now that Bradley has gone, are we still on a sex moratorium?"

"That's just so…romantic…really, Reinhardt."

"Would that be a yes or no?"

"That would be an I'm-still-thinking-about-it."

THE NEXT AFTERNOON, Tansy stirred her soup with one hand and answered the phone with the other.

"Please tell me the grapevine is wrong," Jenna said without preamble.

"I was going to call you but I got on a roll with the book today and just went with it." And she'd known Jenna would flip a gasket.

"Have you lost your mind?"

There went the gasket. "It'll be an adventure. When am I going to get this opportunity again?"

"Hmm. And it doesn't have anything to do with the fact that you're going with Liam?"

"Of course it does. He knows what he's doing. In fact, he and Bull went out or up or whatever you call it with Dalton, looking at it from the plane."

"I know that. Everyone knows everything here. I did not, however, know my sister had signed on for the trip."

"I swear I was going to call you in a bit."

"I'm not worried about that. I'm worried about you. Is it safe?"

"I'm not sure I'd feel safe going with anyone else. Like I said, when will I get this opportunity again? Plus, it was my idea he do this camp thing so it'll be pretty cool to be checking it out."

"I suppose if you're going to do something awful like that, he's the best guy to be with. But better you than me. When are you getting back?"

"Sunday afternoon."

"I'm holding a spot for you for a massage and a mani/pedi on Monday. You're going to need it."

Tansy laughed. "I'm up for all of the above even when I'm not coming in off of a wilderness experience, so thanks. I'm sure I'll be ready for it."

"No doubt. I bet you break at least one nail out there."

"Who knows? Once Liam gets this off the ground, you'll probably be signing up for one of the sessions."

"Sure. When aliens take over my body I'll be right there."

Tansy laughed and a knock sounded on her door. "Gotta run."

"Yeah, Emma's got a dirty diaper over here. Later. But you'd better stop by on your way out tomorrow."

"Will do."

Tansy opened the front door to Liam and her heart thudded against her ribs just at the sight of him.

"What was so funny?" he said.

"Jenna. She thinks I've lost my mind going on this adventure."

Liam grinned and her heart sort of somersaulted in her chest. "She would. I bet she's worried you're going to break a nail."

How'd he know that? "That was exactly what she said."

He leveled a look at her. "Your sister runs a spa and nail salon, of course that's what she'd say."

She almost blurted out that she'd missed him. She didn't realize until right now, with him next to her, just how very much she'd missed him. Her heart felt happy for the first time in a long time…. Actually, her heart had never felt happy this way ever.

Ever practical, Liam said, "Okay, let's take a look at what you've got."

Tansy led him back to where she had her clothes laid out on the end of her bed.

Within seconds he'd reduced her pile by two-thirds. "That's what you need to bring."

"But—"

"No nightgown. You need to sleep in your clothes so you can be ready to roll out at a moment's notice. You only need one extra pair of panties. No bra change. One shirt and one extra pants, three pairs of clean socks and a rain poncho. No makeup. No perfume. Leave everything but your toothbrush here."

Tansy bit back the urge to lobby for some additional items. This was his area of expertise and she'd respect that. "What about a hair brush?"

"A comb would be better. It weighs less and takes up less room."

"Okay, a comb it is."

"You nervous?"

"A little. Mostly excited."

"Want to see a topographical map?"

It was kind of sexy the way that sounded when he said it. "Sure."

Pulling out a map, Liam opened it on the bed. He showed her where they were and where they were going. "See, the great thing about this piece is that it straddles the tree line so you have some barren areas and some wooded areas, which makes for a nice mix of training opportunities."

"I see." What she saw was the way the hair covered his forearm, the way his biceps bunched when he pointed. She ran her finger down his arm. "Speaking of straddling…"

"Oh, yeah?" He grinned and tossed the map to the

top of the pile of clothes on the other side of the bed. He turned and in one swift movement, sat on the bed and pulled her on top of him, which did, in fact, leave her straddling him in intimate proximity.

She linked her arms around his neck. "Yeah." She nipped at his jaw and then his lips.

Gazing at him, realization clicked into place. She loved this man. In one short week she'd found something she'd never had with Bradley, never felt with Bradley. There was nothing conventional or convenient or even seemingly rational about the way she felt about, with or for Liam.

She wasn't ready to say the words and he definitely wasn't ready to hear them. But she could show him.

And she proceeded to do just that with her body... and her heart.

GENERAL WELLINGTON WAS a trouper, he'd hand her that.

"We'll set up camp for the night here," Liam said. It was a nice, small clearing that was relatively flat. They were a decent distance from the stream and would re-cross it in the morning to refill their water, but they were far enough away to keep some distance between themselves and the wildlife that would be drawn to the water.

"Okay." She shrugged out of the pack she'd carried all day and put it on the ground.

Actually, he'd hand her a whole hell of a lot. She hadn't whined or complained all day, even though they'd covered a good bit of ground. Liam was used to operating on his own, but it'd been nice having her along. She was a good person to bounce ideas off of.

"You gather up some firewood while I pitch the tent

and set up the rest of camp. We need small sticks for kindling and bigger pieces to keep it going."

She propped her hands on her hips. "I know that. Sheesh. I was a Girl Scout. Remember?"

Liam laughed. "Okay, Girl Scout, get to it."

"Yessir, sir." She offered a smart-ass grin and a mocking salute as she started reconnoitering the area.

An hour later, Liam passed Tansy a plate of reconstituted beef Stroganoff. "Here you go. The finest in freeze-dried meals."

She took a bite. "Oh, my God, that's good. I didn't expect it to be so tasty."

Liam laughed. "That's what hiking all day will do for you. It wouldn't taste nearly as good if you were sitting in your kitchen at home."

"So, is this what it's like when you're out in the military?"

"In some ways."

"Tell me about it." She smiled at him, her spoon poised over her plate, across the campfire. "You know that's what Girl Scouts do when they camp. They sit around the fire and tell stories."

"Yeah? That's what soldiers do, too. What kind of stories do you want?"

"Whatever you want to tell. If you don't want to talk about the nitty-gritty parts, then just tell me the other."

"The interesting part is that you have these guys who are from different places, different backgrounds, a whole range of personalities, but you're all working toward one common goal." He told her about the guys in his outfit, about Renwald, his spotter who had been his eyes out on missions. Once he started talking, he found he couldn't stop. And it was different from talking to Mallory Kincaid. With Tansy it became personal. He found himself opening up, sharing a part of himself he'd never shared before, not even with Natalie, because Tansy seemed to get him, to understand.

"I like your stories," she said.

"I'm not usually much of a talker."

"You're a good storyteller."

"You're a good listener." He pushed to his feet. "Let's get this cleaned up and the packs in the trees."

"Packs in the trees?" she said as she stood.

"Yeah. We need to clean up away from camp and then hang the packs in the trees to keep out bears and other wildlife. And no food, not even gum or mints, in the tent. Nothing with any scent." He shook his head at her expression. "Guess your troop leader didn't cover that in training, huh?"

She eyed the tree line. "If she did, I forgot. Let's get it done. I really don't want any four-legged visitors."

"Yep. Don't worry. We'll be fine."

They went to the other side of the clearing and into the woods a bit and washed up. Then they backtracked to the other side and he made quick work of rigging their packs up high enough off of the ground and far enough out on a tree. "That should be fine."

Walking back to the camp, she said, "Liam, I have a question."

"Shoot."

She grinned in the descending darkness. "Exactly. Would you teach me to shoot a gun?"

He was only a little surprised by her question. "Have you ever fired a weapon before?"

They were back by the campfire where their tent sat

a short distance from the fire. He sat back down on the log and she did, as well.

She shook her head. "No. I'd like to learn, though."

"Sure. The first thing you need to do is learn about the weapon itself before you do anything else. We could do a basic lesson if you want to."

"That would be awesome."

He unholstered the Glock and took out all the ammunition and then double-checked again that it was empty. "The first rule of thumb is you always handle a weapon as if it's loaded, even when it's not. Don't ever point it at anyone unless you're planning to use it."

He gave her a rundown of the components and basic operation. In the flickering firelight, her gaze was intent. She asked intelligent questions and most importantly, when he handed her the weapon, she wasn't tentative, but she also wasn't careless and cocky.

"You've got a natural grip and you seem pretty comfortable with it," he said.

"It is comfortable. It's not as heavy as I thought it would be."

"Be careful where you're aiming it, but go ahead and practice the grip."

"How's this?" She followed his instructions to a T.

He was impressed. "Not bad, Wellington. In fact, damn good. Is it still comfortable in your hand?"

"I like the way your gun feels in my hand."

She didn't know what she was saying, which made it all the funnier.

"What? What's so funny?"

"There's a saying—this is my weapon, this is my gun. One is for fighting, one is for fun."

A purely sensual smile lit her face and eyes. "Hmm. I

see. Well, I like the way both your weapon and your gun feel in my hand…and the gun in other places, too. In fact, maybe it's time for me to handle your gun again."

"Hand me my weapon." She did, adhering to his safety rules. He reloaded it and put it away while she waited silently. "Now, come here, woman, and handle my gun."

TANSY NURSED A CUP of hot coffee the next morning while Liam cooked breakfast. She was fairly amazed by how well she'd slept considering it was in a sleeping bag on a bedroll on the ground in a tent. She'd felt safe in a tent with Liam. She'd even been okay to get up this morning without a shower and take care of her business behind a bush. All told, she was actually having a great time roughing it.

"I'm pretty happy we made it through the night without being visited by any wild animals."

He grinned at her over the small cookstove. "I don't know. I was pretty into the wild animal in my tent last night. That was fairly spectacular."

"It was, wasn't it? Having fired your gun a couple of times, maybe you could teach me to shoot your weapon if we have some time this morning."

"We could do that. We have time. Now, keep your strength up and eat."

"How much ground do you want to cover today?" They'd hiked about five miles yesterday, which didn't sound like a lot but it had been rugged, somewhat mountainous terrain and they'd been trailblazing. It had been arduous but invigorating.

"We should cover about twelve miles today but it'll be different. We're moving north so once we get through the first three miles or so, we're going to be in much more open terrain with sparse trees. You'll need to layer on your other shirt tonight."

"I'm glad you asked me to come."

"Yeah? We'll see if you still feel that way tomorrow." There was no sting in his words and he grinned. She supposed it was early and they still had a lot of ground to cover. "Let's clean up, break camp, and then we'll get in your firing round before we start."

Half an hour later, Liam looked at her, admiration glinting in his eyes. "You're a quick study, Wellington, and a natural marksman. You sure you never did this before?"

It was ridiculous how good his praise made her feel, and it was all the more meaningful because she knew he wasn't one to hand out praise lightly or blithely. Plus, coming from a man who was one of the best at what he did… "No. Never before."

"Damn good job. Now, you reload the way I told you…that's right…barrel pointing down…yep…now, safety on. Good job. And you remember the most important thing about handling a weapon?"

"Yep. You don't have it if you aren't willing to use it."

"That's right." She passed the weapon to him and he holstered it. "Okay, sharpshooter, ready to march?"

Happiness, contentment and excitement surged through her. Good grief but she loved this man. "Lead on…as long as I don't have to sing cadence."

It was a spectacularly glorious day.

14

THE HAIR ON THE BACK of Liam's neck stood up. Something wasn't right. He couldn't shake a feeling he'd had for a while, and the deal was, when you couldn't shake a feeling, you listened to it because it meant something wasn't right. It had saved his ass more times than he could count.

He didn't want to alarm Tansy but he looked around for an area to take cover. Already the vegetation was less dense, the trees increasingly sparse. According to the topographical map, they were going to be in open terrain in about half a mile and that wasn't feeling safe at this moment.

Something, or someone, was watching them. If it was a friend, they'd have made themselves known by now, which only left him to surmise he was dealing with an unknown foe.

"Let's take a break over here," he said, eyeing a small boulder in a clump of trees. It had become increasingly rocky.

"We can keep going. I'm really not tired."

"We're breaking." He took her hand and steered her none too gently.

Tansy glanced at him. "I was just saying. Okay."

He'd hurt her feelings. It was all in her voice and all over her face. He'd slipped back into full military mode but she was still in aren't-we-having-a-good-time-in-the-woods mode. He had a bad, bad feeling that was all about to change.

His sixth sense, on red alert, led him to grab her and pull her down behind the boulder's cover.

"What are you—"

He'd heard the crack-bang. Any marksman recognized the bang of a rifle being fired and the crack as it impacted its target. The bullet lodged in the tree to their left.

Reflexively, he already had his rifle out and in his hands. "Someone's shooting at us." Actually, the shot had been aimed at Tansy. Had he been the target, the bullet would've landed to the right.

Her eyes widened and the color drained from her face. "What? Why?"

"I don't know why. Do everything I tell you, when I tell you. Got it?"

She nodded mutely. He listened. It was faint, but there. A branch cracked. Based on the shooter's probable position per the entry angle of the bullet into the tree and that crack, he was circling to their left.

Liam motioned Tansy over farther behind the boulder. He unholstered the Glock and passed it to her. She shook her head.

He nodded and pressed it into her hand. "I may need you to back me up and you may need to protect yourself," he said directly into her ear, his voice low. "Just make damn sure you don't shoot me."

A resolution joined the fear in her eyes. Her lips a straight line, she nodded. There was an off chance that the shot had been fired by a hunter who had mistaken them for game. He didn't think so, but he had to cover their bases. To call out wasn't giving away their location, because their location was already known. And whoever had fired that shot was working with a rifle and a scope, which should have given the shooter a clear view. Nonetheless, he wasn't moving them out and being mistaken by some overzealous hunter again.

"Hey," he called out. "Hold your fire. People here."

His words echoed through the woods and were met with nothing but silence. The woods were too sparse for the shooter not to have heard. To get off a shot and have it land that close, and based on the fairly straight entry line of the bullet into the tree, Liam estimated it had been fired from no more than one hundred and thirty-seven meters, definitely close enough for the person to hear him call out.

He scanned the woods through the scope. Nothing. He lowered his rifle. They were going to have to move. It would've been a whole helluva lot easier had he been by himself, or if Tansy was trained personnel. He had worn his BDUs but Tansy was in jeans and a red shirt. He pulled off his pack and yanked out his extra military-issue brown T-shirt, then took her pack off of her back. "Take off your T-shirt and put this on."

Thank God she had the sense not to question him. He reached down and grabbed a handful of dirt, smearing it on his face and arms. He motioned for her to do the same to her face, arms and neck. She did. He shrugged back into his pack.

"We're going to move out now. Leave your pack." He could handle his. Hers would slow her down. Plus, she was only carrying her clothes and sleeping bag. "Stay low. Be as quiet as possible. We're going to backtrack in a zigzag pattern, using the trees and brush as much as possible for cover. Got it?"

She nodded. "I'm scared."

"You should be." She was taking this seriously. She should. Someone was stalking them.

TANSY'S HEART WAS THUMPING so hard she could hear the blood rushing in her ears. Fear like she'd never known before coursed through her, filled her mouth with a bitter metallic taste.

She squatted behind a bush while Liam scanned the area behind them. He pointed to his left and she nodded. Another dash for cover when all she really wanted to do was sit and cower and have this all be over. They made it to their next destination and he motioned for her to drop and stay. Gladly. A bullet whizzed past her to her left. Liam was positioned to her right.

Liam eased into a prone position and pulled out his binoculars. He scanned the woods again. He'd done that each time. His hands were steady. His breathing slow. His face impassive, devoid of any emotion. She was shaking like a leaf. She felt as if she was running a marathon.

She thought about all the things she wanted to do and it wasn't die in the woods in the middle of nowhere. Anger kicked in, tamping back the fear. This was madness. She'd descended into a hell she didn't understand.

Calmly, methodically, he braced his rifle on a branch and used his scope. He positioned himself with one leg under him, his upper body off the ground. It was as if he quit breathing, his body grew so still, and then he moved his finger against the trigger. She jumped at the shot, even though she knew it was coming.

A terrible screeching filled the air.

"Got him," Liam said. "And now I want some answers."

"How do you know it's safe? There might be more than one."

"If there was more than one, we'd be dead. I didn't aim to kill, just to wound. I want answers and a dead man can't talk."

The screeching gave way to sobs and moans. "You can stay here—"

The thought nauseated her. And she was infinitely relieved it wasn't her or him, but was some nameless stranger. Bile rose in her throat and she lay there and puked. Fear, and everything else, spilling out of her as she emptied her stomach. Liam waited, his hand on her shoulder. When she was through he passed her a bandanna. She wiped her mouth.

He sat up and pulled her to him. Fear roiled through her again. "Get back down," she said frantically, trying to get both her and him back to the ground safely. She felt exposed sitting up.

"Do you hear that thrashing? That's someone with a serious injury trying to get away. His trigger arm and hand is disabled. And I want some answers before whoever it is loses too much blood and can't give any answers."

She pulled herself together. "Okay." She handed him back his Glock.

He holstered it. "Once again, follow my instructions. He's wounded, which will make him still dangerous."

They moved fast, Liam with his Glock drawn.

The thrashing had ceased but it wasn't difficult to follow the trail of blood. He motioned her to his left, to take cover behind a tree. The shooter lay propped against a tree, eerily outfitted in camouflage gear, face paint and a camouflage hat. The chest was still moving up and down but the right arm hung useless, blood flowing steadily from a debilitating wound. There was something vaguely, disturbingly familiar about the figure slumped against the tree. At Liam's approach, the shooter looked up.

"She needs to die so we can be together," Mallory Kincaid said, pain and madness shining in her eyes. "I love you."

LIAM WRAPPED THE LAST of Tansy's shredded T-shirt into a makeshift bandage and stood. "She's lost a fair amount of blood but she's young and strong. Her pulse and heart rate are steady, so that's a good sign."

Tansy nodded but said nothing. After her initial horrified expression when it had become clear that Mallory, mentally unstable and clearly obsessed with Liam, had set out to kill her, Tansy had pretty much shut down.

She'd dutifully helped organize the supplies and assisted him in stabilizing the other woman, but she hadn't looked at Mallory and she hadn't spoken other than monosyllabic responses. Acute stress reaction. He'd seen it time and time again.

He put his arms around her and held her close.

"Tansy, it's okay. You're fine. I'm fine. It's all going to be okay."

"What do we do now?"

"Now that she's bandaged, I'm going to secure her to the tree with our rope, just as a precaution. I needed your help stopping the bleeding, but now you can stay away from her. It would probably be best."

Tansy shivered. "The three of us are going to be out here together tonight, aren't we?"

He patiently went over it again with her. At least she hadn't descended into hysteria. "Hopefully not. She needs medical attention. Hopefully they can pick us up north of here, where it opens up."

He got on the two-way and Merilee came back to him. As briefly and concisely as possible, he outlined the situation. He waited while she arranged for an emergency medical chopper.

Tansy sat on the ground, her arms wrapped around her knees, staring in the other direction.

Within minutes Merilee came back with an evacuation ETA and pick-up coordinates. It would be four hours until the medevac helicopter would arrive...and in the meantime Liam and Tansy had to get Mallory to the designated area. It would be too late for her to be portaged out after the chopper arrived.

Liam approached Tansy and explained the situation. "I can rig together a stretcher but I'm going to need your help in transporting her. Are you up to that? If not, I'll manage but if we're working together, it'll keep her stabilized. I understand if it's something you can't do."

For a moment he wondered if she had even heard him as she stared straight ahead. Finally, she turned to look at him, squaring her shoulders as she stood. "Tell me what we need to do."

In fairly short order he and Tansy had fashioned together a stretcher of branches and sleeping bag. He used the other sleeping bag as a blanket. Although it was a warm enough day, Kincaid didn't need to go into further physical shock from her trauma. He secured her to the stretcher with the other rope.

"If you'll carry her feet, I'll take her head." The feet were much lighter and he wasn't even sure that Tansy was going to be up to that. "Use your legs to lift, not your back. Ready? On three. One. Two. Three. Lift."

It was slow going as the terrain was uneven and there was no designated path. Not once did Tansy complain or loosen her grip, although she did request a break a couple of times near the end. Her arms had to be burning with exertion. Mallory Kincaid wasn't overweight, but she was a tall woman with an athletic build—she was no lightweight.

Mallory drifted in and out of consciousness. Tansy remained quiet and Liam simply reassured her they were getting her help. She obviously needed more than medical attention but medical care was his primary objective at this point.

They had reached the clearing and rested about ten minutes when he heard the approaching *thwack-thwack-thwack* of rotors. He stood but Tansy remained seated some distance away from where they'd deposited Mallory.

The chopper touched down and an emergency team disembarked, heading toward Mallory stat. Within minutes they had her loaded onto the helicopter.

Tansy had stood and watched everything unfold from

a distance. Liam approached her now. It was time for her to go.

"Come on, let's get you loaded on the chopper."

She looked at him. "What about you?"

"There's only room for one of us, so on you go."

She shook her head. "I'm not leaving."

"Tansy, be reasonable."

"I came with you and I'm not leaving until you leave." A fierceness pierced the numbness in her eyes.

"I'm used to these kinds of conditions. I'm used to operating alone. I'm ordering you to get on that helicopter."

She crossed her arms over her chest. "And I came with you and I'll leave with you."

He shook his head at the pilot and gave them the liftoff signal.

General Wellington was a helluva woman.

TANSY FELT NUMB, DETACHED. The whole thing had been surreal. No one had ever tried to kill her before. It wasn't a good feeling. The thought was so ludicrous she had to tamp down the hysteria that wanted to surface at the mental understatement.

Liam mercifully interrupted her thoughts. "We need to set up camp, Tansy."

She wanted to do something, needed to do something. "I'll gather firewood."

"Good. I'll pitch the tent."

She walked back to the edge of the woods, suppressing a shudder at all that had unfolded in there. She was grateful—grateful to have something physical to do, grateful that things had turned out the way they had, grateful that she was alive, grateful that she'd stayed behind with Liam rather than leave him, grateful that he thought she was strong enough to move forward and contribute rather than treat her like a helpless invalid.

She picked up sticks for kindling and then rounded up some bona fide firewood. Half an hour later they had a campfire going and dinner was served up.

"What happens next?" she said. The routine and the food was restoring some sense of normal for her.

"The Alaska State Troopers will come out first thing in the morning. They'll want to inspect the scene, gather statements. At some point we'll both have to show up in court."

She nodded and he continued. "Tansy, I had no idea that was what she was thinking. She came on to me at the end of our interview. I turned her down." He shook his head and ran a hand through his hair. "I never led her on. I never touched her."

She sat for a moment, digesting his words. It seemed fairly incomprehensible that Mallory would've gone off the deep end without provocation. However, she believed him. He was a man of integrity, which was a boat Bradley had fallen short of boarding. Then there was the madness glimmering in Mallory's eyes. Shuddering, she nodded, accepting his word as the truth. "I believe you," she said.

"Thank you. You've been through a lot today. I've seen men not handle it as well as you have. You okay?"

"Yeah, I suppose I'm fine." She got up and moved to sit next to him, suddenly wanting, needing, his solid strength beside her. "I guess this…today…was what it was like for you all the time." She had a new appreciation for who he was, what he was, what his job had entailed. How did someone live with that kind of fear, facing death as a part of their job? And yet, that's what men and women in combat did every day, every hour.

"Yes and no. Today it was personal." He slid his arm around her, pulling her hard and tight to his side. She was more than happy to be there. "Especially when I realized you were the target, not me."

"How'd you know?"

"Where the shot landed. It was the tree nearest you. If I'd have been the target, it would've been the one behind me or to my right."

So, he'd known. "Did you have any idea it was Mallory?"

"No. As far as I knew, she left after Bull and I did yesterday. At that point it didn't matter who it was, the person just needed to be stopped. I knew it was someone who had a working knowledge of tactics, but not a lot of practical experience. I also knew it wasn't a professional. It was too personal, based on the number of shots fired. A professional would've sat tight and bided their time to get off a kill shot. She wasn't operating with a cool, detached head and it came through."

Tansy suddenly didn't want to talk about or think about Mallory and her madness. "Tell me about going out on missions."

He talked and she let it wash over her and through her, bringing a new sense of understanding. Of stalking the enemy, but for a cause, a greater purpose, the end result ultimately to save lives by neutralizing the enemy. She didn't ask how many men he'd killed. It didn't matter, except for the toll it might have taken on him.

They cleaned up their dishes, hung the packs and then it was simply the fire, the night sky and the two of them. Tansy came to him and wrapped her arms around his waist, holding him close, her head resting against his chest. She offered him comfort, solace, and sought the same in return.

She was suddenly infinitely grateful for the man he was. He smoothed a hand over her hair, his breath whispering wordlessly against her hair. He laughed softly against her. "This has been a hell of a day and a hell of a trip—certainly not what you'd anticipated. I bet you wish you'd stayed at Shadow Lake."

She didn't have to think about it, there in the shelter of his arms, offering support to him while she took her measure of the same. She stepped back and looked him in the eyes. "No, I don't regret being here. I could be at Shadow Lake now, if I'd wanted to."

"Why didn't you get on that helicopter and leave?"

She shook her head. "I didn't want to leave you," she said.

"I would've been fine."

"I know." He was a lone wolf. A man unto himself. Yet, she'd wanted to stay. Staying had felt right.

And it was as simple and as complicated as that. She'd been operating on adrenaline, numbness, instinct, and she hadn't wanted to leave him. Quite simply, she loved him.

He sighed, twining his fingers in her hair. "You know we don't have any sleeping bags. They went on the chopper."

There'd been no question of transferring Mallory to another stretcher. They'd simply started an IV, assessed her medical state, loaded her on board as she was and left. However, Tansy hadn't actually gotten as far as thinking they were sleeping bagless. And in the big scheme of life and death, it really didn't matter.

"We'll layer on all the clothes we have, put our bed-rolls next to each other and share body heat," Liam said. "It'll get cold tonight but we should be okay in the tent together. I would've never let you stay otherwise."

"I know that."

She realized she trusted him implicitly, with her safety, her life, but more important, with her heart. She hadn't been looking to fall in love with Liam Reinhardt. She hadn't wanted to fall in love with him. But she had.

And in her book love was meant to be shared, to be offered freely, without expecting anything in return, but her heart told her he wasn't ready. He wasn't ready to hear it, to receive it. Plus, there was the little matter that one crazy woman had already declared her love for him today. Tansy figured that was enough for any one man, even one as extraordinary as Liam, in any one given day.

Plus, she knew him well enough, the way his mind worked, that he'd write it off as gratitude or mistaken emotion based on him saving her life. Nope. She knew her own heart. She'd perhaps known it from the moment she'd first seen him but her head and her heart hadn't been ready. And he wasn't ready. For now, she'd hold her own counsel…and love him nonetheless, because her heart hadn't given her any choice in the matter.

15

LIAM WATCHED OUT THE window as the town of Good Riddance came into view. It had been a long night. He'd stayed awake all night, which had felt like being back on alert on a mission, but this time it had been different.

He'd held Tansy, kept his arms around her, keeping her warm, keeping her safe, while it danced through his head over and over just how damn close she'd come to being killed because of him.

He'd done a lot of thinking through the night. He'd never put Natalie first. She'd been right about that. What he'd finally realized last night was that he'd never wanted to put her first, never allowed himself to make that commitment, that leap.

He didn't want anyone to mean that much to him. He could face down the enemy all day, but the thought of allowing someone to mean that much, to matter that much, to be that vulnerable—no. The very idea struck a fear in him that he'd never been willing to acknowledge. He didn't want to be that vulnerable to losing someone. And fast on the heels of that thought had come the thought that what he'd felt for Natalie was a drop in the bucket to what he felt for Tansy.

Tansy *could* mean that much to him, *could* be that important to him *if* he opened himself up to it…and he wasn't going to. He couldn't. He wouldn't. So now she was back in Good Riddance and they could both get on with their lives.

He'd been damn glad when dawn had broken and they'd been busy breaking camp, packing in anticipation of the state troopers' arrival. They'd answered questions, retraced the events of the day before and then all loaded up on the chopper and were touching down now.

Chaos erupted when they cleared the rotors, damn near the whole town turning out to welcome them back. Jenna, her eyes red and swollen from crying, embraced Tansy, holding on to her as if she would never let her go, her husband and their baby right there, as well. Bull, Merilee and Dirk all surrounded Liam. Merilee's tears fell wet against his neck.

"I'm fine," Liam said. "It's over."

Merilee nodded mutely, which spoke volumes for a woman who was always composed with an inner core of steel. He realized Tansy possessed that same inner core of tempered metal.

Dirk clapped him on the back. "That was a hell of a trip, huh?"

Bull stood silently, letting Liam know he'd be there when Liam was ready to talk, when the dust had settled.

Surrounded by the jostling crowd, he felt Tansy's gaze seeking him out. He didn't acknowledge it, didn't acknowledge her. It was time for each of them to move on…in separate directions.

TANSY SETTLED BACK IN the cushioned seat while Jenna worked on her nails. "I knew you'd break a nail, but I didn't expect this. You wrecked your manicure."

"Jenna, do you know how crazy that sounds?"

Her sister grinned. "It does kind of, doesn't it?"

Last night had been a whirlwind of activity and conversation. Merilee had done a great job of keeping the media at bay. Tansy and Liam had each released a statement that essentially said they each had no comment and that had been that. She'd spent a couple of hours on the phone reassuring her mother that she was fine and that no, her mom didn't need to hop on the next plane to Alaska. Jenna had insisted Tansy have dinner with her, Emma and Logan and she'd been more than happy to bask in the safety of their family nest.

Tansy hadn't gotten back out to Shadow Lake until long past dark settling in. She'd seen the lights on next door but knew instinctively that Liam needed some time to himself. And she needed the night to herself, as well. She'd known as surely as she'd known her own name that they each needed their own space to process the past couple of days.

She'd spent the morning immersed in catching up on her work and the afternoon being pampered at Jenna's spa. Ellie had given her the best massage she'd ever had in her life and now Jenna was fussing over her nails. Admittedly, all the pampering felt good.

"I don't want to go back," she said quietly to Jenna.

"Then you can hang out upstairs with Logan and Emma-bug for a while and have dinner with us again."

"No. I mean I don't want to go back to Chattanooga."

A smile blossomed and wreathed Jenna's face. She dropped Tansy's hand and circled the table to hug her.

"You don't know how happy that makes me. I don't want you to go, either. It's been wonderful having you here. I've been hoping and hoping you'd stay. We can talk to Sven about building you a place—"

"I don't want to stay in Good Riddance, either. I will if I have to, but that's not what I want."

Comprehension dawned in Jenna's eyes as she settled back in her seat and once again picked up Tansy's hand. "Liam?"

Tansy nodded. "Yeah. Liam. Do you think I'm crazy?"

Jenna sat, gnawing at her lip, while she filed Tansy's ragged nail. Jenna spoke slowly, obviously choosing her words with care. "I don't think you're crazy, but five days ago you thought you were still in love with Bradley. You know you and Liam just shared a traumatic experience and what you're feeling could be…well, you know, kind of mixed up in your head."

"You make a lot of sense and those are valid concerns. At another point I would've agreed. But I had to work through my feelings for Bradley to see what was in front of my face. I've never been surer of anything. No doubts. Liam, and what I feel for him, feels right in a way Bradley never did. I finally figured out the difference between loving someone and being in love and when you have both…it's just…" She petered out, not even knowing how to put it in words.

She didn't have to. Jenna's smile showed she totally understood. "I get it. Trust me, I get it. And I can see it all over your face. So, how does Liam feel about you?"

"Well, that's still to be determined. He's not an easy man to read and I wanted to give him a little time."

A frown niggled at Jenna's brow. "Not to rain on your parade, Tansy, but I think you need to protect yourself."

She smiled like the fool in love that she was. "It's too late for that, Jenna. Way too late for that. There's nothing quite like being stalked in the woods to make you realize just how short and precarious life is. All I could think about was how much I didn't want to die, all the things I had left undone. And telling Liam I love him, well, I can't in good conscience leave that undone. All I know to do is offer him my heart. I hope he loves me, too. I think we can have a good future together. We work well as a team. For the short period of time we've known each other, I get him and I think he gets me. The only thing I know to do is tell him how I feel. I think he loves me. Maybe he doesn't, but it still doesn't change the way I feel about him. I damn sure hope he loves me because the other thing I know for certain is that he's ruined me for any other man. No one else can compare to him."

"I'll keep my fingers crossed for you, honey. And what's the plan if he's not buying into your plan? Will you go back to Chattanooga then?"

"Nope. No running away, getting away. I'll stay here and get on with my life. I just hope it's with him."

LIAM CAME IN FROM his after-work swim. Finally, things were settling back into a routine. Nothing had changed, yet everything had changed. He'd gone for his run this morning, shown up to work with Sven and moved forward to buy the property.

He went inside, showered and had just finished dressing when he heard her knock at his door. He recognized her knock. Hell, he knew her walk, the way she looked when she was sleeping.

He opened the door and she stood on the other side of the screen door, wearing that dress he liked so much.

She smiled and he steeled himself against the way his body tightened in response. "Hi. Did I catch you at a bad time?"

For a second he thought about saying yes, but instead he stood aside. "Come on in."

She smelled fresh and sweet and against his better judgment, he reached for her, pulling her into his arms, tight against his body. Damn, he'd missed her. The way she felt next to him, her smile, her scent, every damn thing about her.

Wordlessly, she took him by the hand and led him to his bedroom. She slipped her dress over her head. She was naked beneath. He took off the clothes he'd just put on.

Together, they climbed into his bed. There had been something close and intimate in the past night in the woods, when he'd held her wrapped in his arms and stood silent sentinel through the night as she'd slept. And now he told her with his body, with his touch and his kisses, how damn glad he was that she was still part of this earth. But he wouldn't allow her to know how much she meant to him.

Afterward, she propped on one elbow and traced a nothing pattern on his chest with her fingertips. He saw it in her eyes, knew it was coming but couldn't do anything to stop it.

"I love you."

Her words didn't take him by surprise. Funny, but he'd known it, felt it before she'd said it.

"What about Bradley?"

Her eyes pierced him, calling him out. "Evasive

maneuvers, Reinhardt. He went back to Chattanooga. Alone. I made that decision based on me and him. He's a nonissue at this point."

They both knew Liam was in retreat-and-regroup mode. She waited. The next move was his. He wanted to tell her, he almost said it, that they could take it one day at a time, but that wasn't fair to her. She was putting her cards on the table. He owed her the same.

"Tansy, I don't have anything to offer you. I'm just getting back on my feet, starting down a new career path."

She simply looked at him. They both knew that wasn't the issue. "Dammit, Tansy."

He pushed out of the bed and pulled on his jeans. He tossed her dress to her. Her nakedness was distracting.

She pulled on the garment and sat up against his headboard. "I've decided to stay in Good Riddance."

"I haven't asked you to stay."

"No, you haven't. You also didn't ask me to stay when that helicopter was leaving the other night. I stayed then and I'm staying now."

"What are you, some glutton for punishment, Wellington? I can't give you what you want."

"And just so we're on the same page, what is it that you think I want, Reinhardt?"

"What I'm willing to give is what we've got. It works, but that's not going to be enough for you, is it?"

"No. You're right. I'm not going to settle for half measures. I don't care that you're moody and ill-tempered and have the social skills of an armadillo." An armadillo? "I can live with all of that, but I want all of the good parts, too. I want the part that you deny and keep under lock and key. I want the whole man. It's the only way to have a healthy relationship."

"And I'm telling you I'm not a whole man. You want something I don't have to give. Ask my ex-wife."

"I don't have to ask your ex-wife. I know you. I know the heart of you. For such a man of courage, the notion of fully loving someone leaves you quaking in fear and denial. Whether you *choose* to be a whole man, well, that's a different story."

Dammit. She made it sound so easy and there was nothing easy about it. "What are you going to do, Wellington? Move out with me to that remote location? How long do you think that would last? A month? Maybe stretch it to six? I'll be gone for a week at a time. You'll be out in the middle of nowhere alone. You'll see me maybe six days out of a month. How does that fit into your plan?"

She eyed him with cool disdain. "Do you think I'm an idiot? Of course I know that. And it actually sounds great to me. I like a certain amount of alone time. I can always fly in and out with the supply plane when I want some time away. It's not like I'd be in lockdown." She assumed the same stance she had at the sand line. "I want a partner, not a shadow or a hovercraft."

"You've got an answer for everything, don't you, Wellington?"

"Pretty much, Reinhardt. Those six days out of the month that you were home would be good, damn good. And I want a dog."

Why did she have to paint a picture that made it all sound so good? Why couldn't she have just left well enough alone? "Jesus. Next you're going to be throwing in a couple of kids."

She lifted her chin, her eyes unyielding. "In due time. I happen to think you're good genetic material and would make a good dad."

A boy, a girl, one like him, one like her. And what about when the isolation and lifestyle got to be too much and he was way the hell more invested than he'd ever been with Natalie? Hell, he was already more invested than he was with Natalie. No. "So, what is this? A take-it-or-leave-it proposition?"

"On the table."

"And if I can't meet your terms, are you going to leave? Head back to Chattanooga?"

"No. I don't want to leave you, but I also like it here. I like the people. I love my sister and I can be a part of my niece growing up. I'm staying, with you or without you."

"I could come into town in between gigs. We could—"

"No."

"I'm not going to be coerced."

"I'm just leveling with you."

"So much for your profession of love. You don't get your way and suddenly you don't love me."

She laughed and he'd be damned if he saw what was so funny. "No, it'd be nice and tidy if it worked that way but it doesn't. I'm going to love you regardless. My heart didn't leave me any choice in the matter. However, I still have a choice in how I live my life and I'm not settling for half measures."

It reminded him of that damn load of sand she'd had delivered and then drawn her line. "So, I guess you've drawn your line in the sand once again."

"I guess I have."

Damn stubborn woman. She'd see it his way in due time. "Then you stay on your side and I'll stay on mine."

TANSY REMINDED HERSELF that she wouldn't actually expire from a broken heart. She'd hurt like hell but she'd survive. People did it all the time. And the damnable part was she didn't think for a minute he wasn't capable of love. Actually, she didn't think for a minute he didn't love her. And that wasn't arrogance or self-delusion. The tenderness in his touch wasn't just about sex, and it was something she didn't think intensely private men like Liam Reinhardt shared often.

But she couldn't move the man past himself. She'd put it out there and the rest was up to him. In the meantime, she'd get on with her life. She was ever so tempted to cave, to give in, to take what he was willing to give, but she stood firm. She wouldn't settle. Life was too short to settle.

She called Merilee and booked herself a flight out. She had business to attend to in Chatanooga—namely closing out her life there and clearing out her apartment so she could make the move to Alaska. Plus, she wanted to spend some time with her mom. While she wasn't as close to her dad, she wanted to at least have dinner with him. She was ready to move on with a new phase of her life.

And a woman could always hope that the man of her heart would stop being an idiot and come through.

She parked the FJ Cruiser at Jenna's and her sister met her at the door. "Emma-bug and I will see you off. You want her or you want me to carry her?"

"I'll take her."

With a smile, Jenna handed over the flannel sling

that went around Tansy's neck and then placed Emma in the pouch. The sleeping baby grunted and nestled closer in the fabric, next to Tansy's midsection, and kept sleeping. Tansy welcomed Emma's warmth and weight against her.

Together they walked down the street. Quietly, Jenna reached for and held her hand. "It'll all work out in the end, Tansy. Give him some time and you know we'll be waiting here for you."

"I know. I'll be back in a month."

They walked into the airstrip office to find the regulars there—Alberta, Lord Byron, Dwight, Jefferson, Bull and Merilee. Liam wasn't there. She hadn't expected him to be there. Nonetheless, she had hoped. He knew she was leaving and he'd steadfastly kept his distance. He hadn't answered her knock on the door last night when she'd stopped by to say goodbye. She supposed he figured they'd said everything there was to say.

Merilee smiled and took Emma. "Here's my girl." She looked at Tansy. "We'll have you all set up when you get back. Don't you worry, honey, we'll have a place for you to stay other than Shadow Lake."

Housing was an issue in the small town and while she'd enjoyed the accommodations at Shadow Lake, she couldn't continue to live next door to Liam for a number of reasons. One being, the cabins at Shadow Lake were temporary and Skye's folks were coming in for a visit in November. Plus, she wanted a fresh start and there were too many memories there. It would be too easy to fall into and settle for whatever Liam was willing to give.

There were a couple of options on the table—

sharing the apartment above Gus's with Ruby, the wait-ress who was staying there, staying with Jenna and her family, and there were a couple of other things Merilee and Bull were working on. Of course, she was hoping it was a matter of none of the above and Liam came to his senses.

"I know," she said to Merilee.

Alberta patted her hand. "It's all going to be fine. I knew when you sent that Bradley fellow packing, you were going to be A-OK. No hooking up with him while you're in Chattanooga." She cackled at her own joke, coaxing a smile out of Tansy.

"Not even a remote possibility."

Bull, standing quietly in the background, as was his way, caught her eye. "Time, Tansy. Give him time. It has a way of letting things unfold."

Tansy nodded, holding Bull's words close to her heart, finding comfort in them, even more than any-thing anyone else could say to her now. Bull knew Liam as well as anyone.

Juliette came in the back door, Baby in tow. "Okay, we're ready if you're ready. There's a storm blowing in but we should beat it out."

Tansy hugged her goodbyes and crossed the airstrip. She'd be back. She had no choice. Her heart was here.

16

"I OUGHT TO KNOCK the hell out of you again," Dirk said, without any hint of animosity as he, Liam, Sven and Bull gathered around rough drawings on Bull's counter in the hardware store. They were designing the main building for Liam's survival camp.

"Then you damn well better make it good, because I'm going to swing back this time."

Unperturbed, Dirk shrugged. "Well, hell, someone's got to knock some sense into you."

"You're trying my patience, Dirk."

The big man laughed. "You've got to be kidding. Like you haven't been trying everyone's patience for the past month. You're like a damn bear with a sore paw."

"Mind your own business."

"It is my business. I have to work with your sorry ass and you are one miserable son of a bitch, and since shit rolls downhill, I'm catching yours."

Bull spoke up. "The man has a point."

Attempting to get back to business, Sven wisely changed the subject. "We should do what we did on

Jenna's place and build up with a little more room to accommodate family quarters."

Liam considered Sven's suggestion. It'd be tight, but he should be able to swing it.

And damnation, he missed Tansy. The woman haunted him. Her smile, her voice, the sex—he even missed their quiet talks while sitting around the fire pit behind the cabin. And she was smart. More than once he'd wanted to know what she would've thought about the plans—he'd have liked her input. But there was that line in the sand and she'd laid out the terms of crossing it.

So, here he sat, one miserable son of a bitch. Dirk had called that right, being dogged out by the three of them. It'd been the longest month of his life…and now she was back. He'd caught a glimpse of her in Gus's. Then there'd been another "sighting" when he'd been on his way to Bull's for this meeting, but they'd each taken and were holding their positions. General Wellington had dug in. He'd sort of thought it'd be better once she was back, but really it was worse.

When she was gone, there was distance separating them. Now, the only thing separating them were her terms, which required unconditional surrender. She was a most unreasonable woman…and a damn fine general…considering she was outflanking him and out-maneuvering him.

He looked at Sven. "Do I want to know the odds?"

Sven was known to follow Rooster's betting and Liam had known for some time he and Tansy were the biggest bet going.

The big blond grimaced, his eyes sympathetic.

"They're weighted pretty heavily. You're a long shot at this point."

He eyed the three of them. "You all got money riding on this?"

At least they had the decency to look sheepish. Bull? Even Bull? His uncle shrugged. "Hey, I had to throw a couple of bucks at it."

"So, you've all got a vested interest."

Dirk laughed. "Hell, no. It's weighted so heavily in Tansy's favor, the most I'm going to pick up is a couple of bucks."

They all eyed him with a mixture of pity and amusement, as if they knew he was fighting a losing battle but were humoring him nonetheless. "I've lived through firefights where the odds were stacked against me."

Dirk rolled his eyes. Sven laughed. Bull clapped him on the back. "Opening doors, son, opening doors. Sometimes you've just got to lay down your weapon and surrender your gun."

The subtlety wasn't lost on him. Bull winked. "It worked out well enough for me. I set siege for twenty-five years."

"Look," Sven said, as if reasoning with a simpleton. "I thought I'd never settle down and look at me. Juliette's the best thing that ever came my way. And I damn near lost her."

Dirk wasn't about to be left out. "I had my head up my ass and let you waltz Natalie right out from under me. By the way, I talked to her last week."

He'd had enough. He pushed back from the table, standing. He reached in his pocket and pulled out a Ben Franklin and tossed it on the table in front of Dirk. "You've got five minutes to get that to Rooster."

"You can't bet on yourself," Dirk said.

"I'm not, dammit. Put the money on Wellington."

He pulled on his jacket and walked down the street to the airstrip, beelining for Merilee. "I need something white," he said, cutting straight to the chase. "Anything."

Merilee grinned and walked over to the table beside the love seat and picked up a lace doily. "That's the best I can do for you. That or underwear."

"I'll take this."

"She's at Jenna's."

He wasted no time heading back down the street.

TANSY HEARD HIS FOOTSTEPS on the stairs leading to Jenna's house. She had time to utter one word to her sister before his knock at the door. "Liam."

Jenna smiled. "I'll just step into the bedroom."

"You don't have to."

"Oh, yes, I do."

Tansy opened the door and silently stood aside for him to enter. He walked in, past her and tossed something on the table. A white lace doily?

He faced her, back straight, shoulders up. "You sighted me in your crosshairs the moment I met you. I have been outmaneuvered, outflanked and outranked. I concede the firefight, Wellington."

"You are the most unromantic man I know."

"True." He stood unyielding. He nodded toward the white lace. "I surrender."

"You know the terms."

"We need to negotiate those."

She crossed her arms over her chest, holding her line. "Let's hear them."

"Two dogs. Three kids."

She waved a dismissing hand. "That's never been the sticking point."

"I suppose you want a ring on your finger."

"It'd be nice, but I'm still waiting."

"You don't give a man any quarter, do you, Wellington?"

"There's not a lot of room for negotiation on the major term."

He stood there, tall and proud, and she waited, her heart thumping in her chest. He was a man of integrity. A man of his word. He wouldn't give it lightly, which made it all the more important.

"I love you." The words hung between them. "All of me. Heart, body, soul, I'm yours."

She wanted to ask if it'd really been that hard to say, but she didn't have to. She knew it had. "Thank you. I love you, too. I'll stand by you, with you."

She picked up the lace doily and handed it back to him. "I don't need this. The way I see it, it's not surrender at all, we're just combining forces. We've always been on the same side, Reinhardt. You just needed to figure it out."

"Come here, woman."

She willingly, eagerly, stepped into his arms, kissing him with all the passion and longing she'd kept to herself for the past month, week and two days—and yes, she'd counted. She felt the same thing in his kiss...and much more. His lips silently spoke of promise and a future and a here and now beyond compare.

He rested his forehead against hers. "It's going to take time for me to get this off the ground. I think it'll work, but it's not going to be easy. I don't have anything to offer you, honey, except for a lot of hard work."

"The things worth really having usually aren't easy.

God knows, you haven't been. But we'll travel that path together and you've offered me everything—you and a future together. How did I get so lucky?"

He shook his head. "I've been asking myself the same thing. I guess doors have opened while others have closed, while our paths have led to each other's."

"Are you getting philosophical and sentimental?" she asked.

"I have my lapses." He looked down at her, his eyes glittering with a look she had longed for on all her lonely nights since they'd been apart. "Now why don't you leave that dress on, but—"

"Liam—" She stopped his wandering hand.

"Tansy?"

"Jenna's in the other room."

"Hi, Liam," Jenna said, poking her head out the door. "Welcome to the family."

"Thanks. I'm going to take your sister now. She has building plans to look over."

Jenna laughed. "Okay. Her suitcase is here, though."

"We'll come back for her things later," he said, already ushering her toward the door. She could feel the sexual tension radiating from him. He was as ready for her as she was for him.

"He's in charge," she said to Jenna over her shoulder as they walked out the door.

She wrapped her arm around his waist, feeling the quiet strength of her strong man. At least she'd let him think he was in charge. It just worked better that way.

* * * * *

A sneaky peek at next month...

Blaze.

SCORCHING HOT, SEXY READS

My wish list for next month's titles...

In stores from 16th November 2012:

☐ Red-Hot Santa — Tori Carrington

& Lead Me Home — Vicki Lewis Thompson

☐ The Mighty Quinns: Kellan — Kate Hoffmann

& Feels So Right — Isabel Sharpe

Available at WHSmith, Tesco, Asda, Eason, Amazon and Apple

Just can't wait?

1112/14

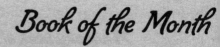

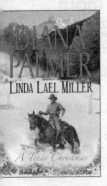

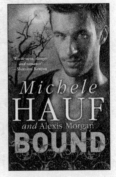
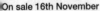

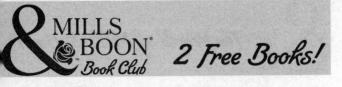